KILLING

AT

COTTON

HILL

A SAMUEL CRADDOCK MYSTERY

A
KILLING
AT
COTTON
HILL

TERRY SHAMES

SEVENTH
STREET
BOOKS™

59 John Glenn Drive
Amherst, New York 14228–2119

Published 2013 by Seventh Street Books™, an imprint of Prometheus Books

Cover image © Media Bakery
Back cover image © PhotoDisc
Cover design by Grace M. Conti-Zilsberger

Inquiries should be addressed to
Seventh Street Books
59 John Glenn Drive
Amherst, New York 14228–2119
VOICE: 716–691–0133 • FAX: 716–691–0137
WWW.PROMETHEUSBOOKS.COM

17 16 15 14 13 • 5 4 3 2 1

Library of Congress Cataloging-in-Publication Data

Shames, Terry.
   A killing at Cotton Hill : a Samuel Craddock mystery / by Terry Shames.
      pages cm
   ISBN 978-1-61614-799-0 (pbk.)
   ISBN 978-1-61614-800-3 (ebook)
      1. Ex-police officers—Fiction. 2. Women—Crimes against—Fiction.
3. Texas—Fiction. I. Title.

PS3619.H35425K55 2013
813'.6—dc23

                                                                    2013010149

Printed in the United States of America

For David

CHAPTER 1

I watch Loretta Singletary hurry up the steps to my house. She hasn't seen me on the porch in my beat-up old rocker where I often sit to catch any early morning breeze. Usually Loretta doesn't miss a thing, so I know she's on a mission. So as not to scare her, I start rocking and clear my throat. She jumps anyway, like a weasel has crossed her path.

"Samuel, you liked to've scared me to death," she says.

"Well, I didn't mean to," I say. "You've got something on your mind, otherwise you would have seen me."

"I do, and it's terrible news. Let me get a drink of water and I'll tell you about it." She opens my screen door. "You want anything?"

I tell her no. She steps lively down the hall, across the linoleum of the kitchen, opens the refrigerator door, and pours herself a glass of water.

I've got uncanny hearing for a man in his sixties, which is why I can hear every move she makes. Loretta doesn't hear as good as me, but she still has a brisk bounce in her walk. I've known Loretta so long I hardly pay attention to what she looks like anymore, but the bare facts are she's short and a little on the plump side, with gray hair that she keeps in tight curls like a halo around her face, and pale blue eyes. She always had nice legs, and they are still her pride, so she wears skirts and disapproves of women who wear pants. She's been a good friend to me since my wife died, though we're not as attached as she'd like to be.

Back out on the porch, she's so agitated that she jerks this way and that as she settles in. "You know Dora Lee Parjeter, lives out in Cotton Hill? She was found murdered this morning."

I feel like somebody punched me in the gut. Dora Lee called me last night, way after I was in bed—I often get to bed before dark in the summer, because I'm up so early. She was just about hysterical and told me she thought somebody was spying on her. After her husband died ten years back, Dora Lee was nervous being out on the farm by herself, and she used to call me, imagining someone was lurking around. I spent a number of years as chief of police, and some people never got out of the habit of depending on me to sort out such things.

After her grandson, Greg, came to live with her, Dora Lee wasn't so afraid anymore, so I was surprised a couple of weeks ago when she called me with the idea that somebody was sitting on the road leading to her farm keeping an eye on the place. I told her the same thing I always used to tell her: "Dora Lee, if you're still worried tomorrow morning, you call me and I'll see what I can find out."

That usually worked pretty well to settle her down in the past, but I'd had the devil of a time last night convincing her that she'd be okay. Turns out she was right and I was wrong.

"I suppose I better go on out there," I say.

Loretta stares at me like I've grown a second head. "What do you want to go out there for?"

"Loretta, if somebody killed you, would you want Rodell to be the person trying to figure out what happened?" Rodell Skinner is the chief of police.

"I guess you're right, but what's that got to do with you?"

"I've got good sense."

I head into the house for my hat and my cane and the keys to my truck. There's not a thing wrong with me but a bum knee. Several months ago one of my heifers knocked me down accidentally and it spooked her so bad that she stepped on my leg. This happened in the pasture behind my house, where I keep twenty head of white-faced Herefords. It took me two hours to drag myself back to the house, and those damned cows hovered over me every inch of the way.

When I get back outside, Loretta is in the truck. "What do you think you're doing?" I ask.

"You're not going out there without me." I know better than to argue with Loretta when she gets that tone of voice.

Heading out of town I ask her how she came to find out the news that Dora Lee was dead.

"Ida Ruth called me. One of Rodell's men told his wife, and she called Ida Ruth." Ida Ruth and Dora Lee are best friends. They get teased because they've both got double names.

"I suppose Ida Ruth will be out there at the house."

"No, she was on her way to Waco for a church conference. She won't be back until tomorrow afternoon. She was awful upset, but she said there's no way she could get out of it." The Baptist preacher may think he runs the church, but he just thinks so because Ida Ruth lets him.

Loretta keeps clearing her throat.

"Well, out with it," I say.

"Ida Ruth says Rodell's pretty sure he knows who did it. He said Dora Lee's grandson probably got it in his mind that he'd be better off with her money than with her."

"And we all know how much Rodell's opinion is worth," I say.

"That's not all. Ida Ruth said Dora Lee and the boy had an argument last week."

"That doesn't mean he'd kill her." I don't like all this jumping to conclusions.

"Who else would have done it?"

"We'll have to see about that."

Cotton Hill, where Dora Lee's farm is located, is a tiny hamlet roughly halfway in between Jarrett Creek and the county seat, Bobtail. It's high summer and the drive out to Cotton Hill is pretty, the alfalfa thick on the ground, the post oak trees still green from the wet June we had. And the cotton is just a few weeks from ready to pick. It's a terrible crop for the land, sucking up all the nutrients and leaving it as depleted as if it had been strip-mined, but it makes a pretty sight as we cut down the county road to Dora Lee's farm.

I turn onto the gravel road that leads up to Dora Lee's little house, and Loretta crosses her arms tight against her chest. "You seem to be mighty familiar with the way out here."

"Been out here to see Dora Lee a time or two," I say.

Before she can pick at me anymore, we pull into the driveway to the side of the house and park behind three vehicles, including a Texas Highway Patrol car. Since homicides occur so seldom around here, every law enforcement body wants to get in on the action. All of a sudden, Dora Lee's murder looms up real to me, and I feel a flash of outrage toward whoever did such a terrible thing. When I climb out of my pickup, I wipe my sweaty hands on my pants.

There's a clump of people standing in the yard. Besides Rodell and one of his lieutenants, the Baptist preacher is there, standing with hands clasped over his belly and a sour look on his face. The two highway patrolmen are wearing their hats and sunglasses like they think a TV crew is going to come barreling up any second and they want to be sure they look the part.

Dora Lee's grandson, Greg, is standing off to one side scratching at a raw place on his chin. A scrawny youngster of about twenty, Greg came to stay with Dora Lee three years ago after his folks, Dora Lee's daughter Julie and her husband, died in a car accident. He and Dora Lee got on well, but I've always found him a little pleased with himself.

Everybody turns and watches Loretta and me walk over to join them, their expressions as wary as if they've been caught doing something wrong. The preacher's face is fire-red in the heat.

"Chief, how you doing?" Rodell says. I can smell whiskey on his breath, left over from last night. He still calls me Chief from when I had his job. That was in the days when it was an elected position. Now it's an appointment made by the county sheriff, Rodell's cousin.

Rodell's just under six feet, with rangy arms and legs and a big old beer gut that hangs over his belt. He's recently grown himself a little mustache that he's fond of stroking, and wears mirrored sunglasses so you see yourself reflected in them.

"I'm doing okay," I say. "I was surprised as hell to hear about Dora Lee. I wanted to come out here and find out what happened."

My eyes flick to the two patrolmen. One of them has a toothpick stuck in the side of his mouth. I can't see his eyes behind the sunglasses, but the way he's faced I can tell he's looking straight at me. I nod at him, and he turns away to confer with his partner, too busy or important to be polite.

"Dora Lee was stabbed, but that's about all we know," Rodell says. "We're waitin' on Doc Taggart to get out here."

I start to ask if I can go in and see her, which I bet he'll say no to, but about then another car drives up. It's the doc, and he hollers for someone to come help him get his gear out of the back. While they're all concentrating on that, I slip away and around the side of the house. Dora Lee's house is small, so I don't have far to go, but I'm hustling fast because I don't have much time to get a look at things before they shoo me out. As I walk, I scan the ground to see if I can make out any footprints, but with this drought we've had, the ground is hard-packed and not likely to yield information.

I step up off the back steps into the kitchen and wait while my eyes get adjusted from the bright light outside. I slip the clip-on shades off my glasses and put them in my shirt pocket. When she died, Dora Lee slid down the cabinet, coming to rest slumped against it, with one leg at a cockeyed angle. She's staring straight at me like she's mad I didn't come out here last night and stop this from happening. I take off my hat and hold it to my chest. Someone, most likely one of the highway patrolmen, has strung some yellow crime scene tape in a rough rectangle from kitchen counter to a chair, to another chair and back to the counter. I can't imagine Rodell having the foresight to bring the tape.

Time was, Dora Lee was a good-looking woman with a fine figure. She's put on a little weight and her dark hair has gone to gray, but she still has those deep brown eyes that made her such a popular girl when we were in school together. I had a crush on her and went out with her a time or two. A torrent of water has gone under the bridge since those days.

Even after Dora Lee was a widow, I never saw her when she wasn't dressed nice. She needed glasses, but she refused to wear them, out of vanity, except for reading and quilting. There are those who think she put on airs for a country girl, but my wife, Jeanne, always said she admired women who didn't let themselves get dowdy.

I tear my eyes away from looking at Dora Lee's face and concentrate on the mess that's been made of the front of her clothes. She was killed before she had time to get comfortable for the night. She's wearing blue slacks and a white blouse. Or, at least, it was white. Blood has spilled down the front and puddled in her lap. The knife, a vicious-looking Bowie knife with a hefty handle and wide blade, is still there, sticking out of her chest. And there is more than one stab wound. Whoever did this wanted to be sure they made a thorough job of it. I don't think Dora Lee would have such a knife in her possession, so whoever killed her must have brought it with him. The blood has darkened, so the wounds are many hours old. A fly has made its way into the house and is buzzing around her. My stomach gives a little lurch and I look away.

For the first time, I wonder where Skeeter is, and if he set up a fuss when whoever killed Dora Lee came in. Skeeter is the latest in a long string of temperamental collies. Dora Lee never would have any other kind of dog. Skeeter should have escorted me around the outside of the house when I arrived. They must have put the dog somewhere so it wouldn't get in the way, but I don't hear any commotion like I should if he's penned up.

I take in the details of the kitchen, the dishes washed and in the drainer—two of everything, so Greg must have eaten dinner with her. Come to think of it, I never knew Dora Lee to leave the dishes to drain. She would have dried them and put them away. So she must have been killed between the washing and the drying. That could be a problem for young Greg, especially given what Ida Ruth said about the two of them having a fight last week.

I hear voices coming around to the back, so I take one more quick look around the kitchen, stopping when I get to Dora Lee. "Goddamn," I say softly, "I'm sorry as hell." Then I hustle on into the front part of the house. I turn left and go into her bedroom. Neat as a pin, it's plain but pretty. She made the handsome quilt on the bed herself, and her son-in-law painted the stodgy picture of her house that hangs over the bed. On the bureau there are framed photos of Dora Lee's husband, Teague, and several of her daughter Julie and her husband, the ones who died in the car accident. There's only one of her other daughter, Caroline, as a little girl.

I pick up a faded photo of the Grand Canyon with an old Ford in the foreground. Dora Lee was so proud of that picture. She and Teague took their honeymoon there. She always talked about going back but never made it. Seems like that no-good rascal Teague could have at least done that much for her.

I poke my head into the bathroom, but as far as I can tell everything is where it ought to be. Not that I'd know if something in particular was out of place, but it looks tidy anyway. Then I move on up to the front bedroom. I can hear Loretta in the kitchen giving orders about how things ought to be done. I'll bet that's going over big with Doc Taggart. He's a prissy SOB who thinks because he has an MD he's right up there next to God almighty and everybody ought to treat him that way.

Opening the door to the second bedroom, I'm hit by the heat. With the door closed, the air-conditioning hasn't reached in here. The room presents a challenge. Dora Lee spent most of her time quilting, and the room is packed with bags of fabric, rolls of bunting, and partly-pieced sections of quilts. I wouldn't be able to tell whether somebody came in and rummaged around looking for something, because it has always been a mess. "Samuel," Dora Lee told me, "everybody's got to have a room they can just let go. I can shut the door to the room and sort things out when I please." From the looks of it, she hasn't pleased in quite a while.

I take a good look around. One thing catches my eye right away. There's a place on the wall where a picture used to be. You can see the paint has faded around where it hung. I wipe my finger over the area that was covered by the picture. My finger comes away clean, so it hasn't been gone long. I close my eyes and try to remember what the picture looked like. I think it was some kind of landscape, but I can't come up with anything more than that.

Somebody is walking as quiet as they can, sneaking up behind me. Probably thinks because I'm old I can't hear. "Sir, what are you doing in here?"

I don't turn around. I know it's going to be that highway patrolman with the bad manners. "I knew Dora Lee for a long time, and I'm paying my respects."

"I have to ask you to leave the house," he says. "This is a crime scene. I'm sure you'll have time when we're done to come back." He isn't unkind, just stiff.

"I'll be on my way," I say. To avoid the crowd in the kitchen, I leave by the front door. In all the voices I heard talking in the kitchen, I didn't hear the boy, Greg. He lives in a shed behind the house. That wasn't Dora Lee's doing. Dora Lee wanted him to live in the house, but the boy insisted on taking over the shed. It took him several months to convert it into a living space. I've never seen the inside of it, but Dora Lee said he made a right nice place out of it.

I walk back around the house and make my way to the shed. When I'm close to it, I see that it's been converted into a compact little cabin. I wonder if the boy did all the work himself.

I tap on the door and hear him moving around inside, and after a minute he opens the door. His eyes are red and his look is hopeless, a far cry from the arrogant face he usually presents. "Yes sir?" A pungent smell of turpentine wafts out through the open door, reminding me that Dora Lee said the boy wanted to be an artist, a claim I never took seriously.

"I hate to bother you," I say, "I just want to make sure you're all right. Can I come in?"

Greg looks over his shoulder, then back at me, and shrugs. He looks younger than his years, having yet to fill into his body. His jeans hang on his hips and skinny arms stick out of a ratty old T-shirt covered with colored smudges. With an unruly mop of hair, and his face long and bony, he's not an attractive boy. He steps back to let me inside, and I enter another world.

My wife, Jeanne, was crazy about modern art. She grew up in Fort Worth, where some of the best museums in Texas are located, and she was hooked on it. She dragged me to galleries with her, and it turned out I liked looking at art almost as much as she did. Before I met her, I liked pictures of bluebonnets and cactus, but she got me fired up about abstract painters.

So I have some knowledge of art, and I know the minute I walk into the room that I should have paid more attention to Dora Lee's talk of the boy's dreams. What is it that makes people think great artists have to come from somewhere else?

The walls are covered with his paintings, and they are stacked against the floorboards. The room is so crowded with tables containing all the paraphernalia that an artist works with—jars of brushes, tubes of oils, sketchbooks, tape, and piles of paint-smeared rags—that there is barely room for the single bed. As Greg sits down on the bed and gestures for me to take a straight-backed chair nearby, I notice that his hands are covered with pastel dust.

My pulse has speeded up at the sight of all this artwork that has been going on right under my nose, and me not paying a bit of mind to it.

"Sorry it's a little messy in here," he says. He darts a look at me and then away, to see how I'm responding to what I see there.

"All right with you if I take a look?" I say.

He shrugs. "I'm just learning."

Just learning. The way Kandinsky and de Kooning and Diebenkorn "just learned." Taking raw talent, and from the look of it, working all hours to mine that talent. He paints with the colors of what he sees right here in his world; earth and dark loam and rust-colored iron deposits; the endless varieties of greens of grass and leaves; and the whole palette of sky colors we get around here from stark blue to stormy grays and greens to sunset blazes. All the things I love about this part of the country. What he does with those colors is a miracle. Most of the work is small scale, and I think he could benefit from spreading it out a little on a larger canvas. On a homemade easel he's begun work on a pastel of storm grays with a faint undercurrent of rose.

"You're doing some good work," I say, tearing my eyes away, my heart beating hard. Greg is looking at me with kind of barely tolerant amusement, as if he can't imagine I'd know anything about what he's up to. I think of the tacky little painting over Dora Lee's bed done by Greg's daddy, and wonder how such a gift came of that. I despair that Dora Lee hadn't a clue that the boy was doing anything more than dabbling. "I'm sorry about your grandmother," I say. "You have any idea what happened?"

He hunches forward, elbows on his knees and shakes his head.

"Were you the one who found her?"

He looks up at me, suddenly wary, and I suspect that Rodell has already scared him into thinking he's a suspect. "No sir, Mrs. Underwood from the next farm down came over this morning. I heard her screaming." His voice wobbles suddenly.

I wait while he composes himself. "Your grandmother was proud of you," I say. "You know she was glad to have you here."

"I know."

I hesitate, wondering if I should tell him Dora Lee called me last night. Maybe that's not the best idea. "You didn't hear anything last night to make you think something was wrong?"

"Of course I didn't!" He gets up abruptly, and his fists clench. "You think I would have just stayed out here and let her get killed?"

"Son, settle down. I just mean that sometimes we hear things and we don't even know we're hearing something important. Like a car driving up into the driveway, or somebody laughing, or the dog barking. By the way, where is Skeeter?"

He shoves his hands into his pockets. "We had to put Skeeter down last week."

"What happened?" He wasn't old, so I know it must be something else.

"He got into something that made him sick and they couldn't do anything for him at the vet's."

"That's a damn shame." I'm trying to figure out how to give the boy a little comfort when there's a loud knock on the door. Before he can get to it, the door is flung open. Rodell strides in flanked by the two highway patrolmen. "Boy, you need to come with us," he says.

Greg's eyes widen and he steps back. "Why?"

"We need to take you down to the station and ask you some questions."

The boy looks around at his safe nest. "Can't you ask me here?"

"No, we can't. Now come on with us."

Greg backs up another step. The two patrolmen are poised to grab him, so I step up near him. "Look at me, son."

He looks, and I see a terrified calf.

"It's going to be okay. You don't have anything to be afraid of." I'm hoping I'm right, but I know that the reason Rodell barged in here to take this boy away was to get Dora Lee's murder wrapped up quick. He's not going to attend to the finer points of whether or not the boy is guilty. Greg is convenient, that's the important thing.

One of the patrolmen snickers, but I hold the boy's eyes with mine. I'm promising him, and I see the promise take hold.

CHAPTER 2

Loretta is in a state of indignation, and for the first five minutes of our drive back to Jarrett Creek she keeps her mouth firmly closed. That's fine with me, because I'm trying to sort out the steps I need to take to get the boy released. But the silence can't last, and pretty soon words start to tumble out, like what did I think I was doing sneaking around back there, just how well did I know Dora Lee? "I always thought it was crazy for her to live out on that farm by herself. And now look what's happened!"

"She wasn't by herself," I say. "She had her grandson there."

"A lot of good it did her! And it looks like he's probably the one who killed her anyway. Like Ida Ruth said, he's probably looking for her inheritance."

"You told me Ida Ruth said they had an argument. Did she say what it was about?"

"The boy wanted to get a job, and Dora Lee told him there was plenty to do around her place."

Dora Lee had told me Greg was thinking he might have to move to Houston if he couldn't find a job around here, but that was several weeks ago. "Well, it seems to me that if he was willing to work, he's not somebody who'd kill his grandmother for money. Besides, the two of them got along well with each other."

"And how do you know so much about it, anyway?"

One problem with being a widower is that old women have us outnumbered. Right after Jeanne died I was scandalized and soon terrified at how quickly women started sniffing around. I'm no Gregory Peck. I'm not saying I've let myself go completely. I work outdoors taking care of the cows, so I've kept trim and I've got all my hair. But the hair is streaked with silver, my blue eyes are surrounded by wrinkles and my jowls have sagged down, so I look like a hound.

But I guess to ladies of a certain age, just having a member of the opposite sex to lean on is good enough. Most of them gave up after a while, realizing I wasn't in the market for a new wife. But Loretta is one of those persistent ones. Truth is, I don't mind her most of the time. She and I can sit down on an afternoon and play a game of gin rummy and sip a glass of something and have a good old time. What I don't like is when she starts thinking she has a hold on me.

"I've known Dora Lee as long as you have, Loretta. Longer. We lived on the same street when we were babies. You didn't come to Jarrett Creek until third grade."

"Second grade."

"After Teague died, Dora Lee came to depend on me. I didn't mind helping her out time to time."

There's a lot I'm not saying, because it's information Dora Lee would have been ashamed to have bandied about as gossip. Fact was, Teague was mean as a rabid dog. He used to knock Dora Lee around, and when she was scared, she'd call me. I don't think it was herself she was so scared for, but her daughters. Jeanne never said a word when I'd get in my pickup in the dead of night and head out there to make Teague behave. Dora Lee knew that Jeanne could have kept me home and she appreciated that Jeanne let it alone. When Jeanne got sick, no one helped out more than Dora Lee. By then Teague had been dead several years.

"So you got to know the boy, too?" Loretta says.

"No, not really. He pretty much made himself scarce."

"Standoffish, probably, the way young boys will get." Loretta has two boys, long grown and out of the house, so she knows something about them.

But after seeing all Greg's paintings in his cabin, I'm thinking something else made him keep to himself. He was obsessed with his art.

We're almost at my place, and I can't put up with Loretta anymore right now. I've got too much on my mind, so I stop in front of her trim little house. It's just down the way from mine. She gives me a look that's all pinch-mouthed and narrow-eyed. I don't have time to appease her. I'm worried about that boy. Well, not the boy so much as his art, if you can separate the two things. I climb out and go around to open the door for her, and she has no choice but to get out of the truck.

"I'll see you later," I say to her rigid back, as she marches up the sidewalk to her house.

At home I make myself a cup of coffee and sit down with the telephone. I don't have to call my nephew, but I'll take any excuse to talk to him. I'm in luck and he's not in court today, so his secretary comes back on and says he'll call me back in a few minutes.

I sit back and take pleasure in the anticipation. Tom is my brother Horace's only child, and a better man you couldn't hope to find. I sometimes think Tom was dropped into the wrong family. He's always busy with something, interested in what goes on in the world, wanting to make his way—more like me than my brother, truth be told. Horace came out of the womb surly and stayed that way. Wanted things thrown in his lap, never worked for something he couldn't find a way to get for free. He and his wife lived in a trailer on the outskirts of town and he was pushed out of shape that I had made something of my life. He's long dead, and although I feel guilty saying so, the world didn't lose much when they put him in the ground.

By the time Tom was about ten, he'd figured out that he had more fun here with Jeanne and me than at home. It suited Jeanne and me; disappointed as we were that we couldn't have children of our own. I guess it suited his folks, too, for him to hang around most afternoons after school. And when he wanted to go off to college and law school, I took it as a natural thing that I'd help him pay for it. I've gotten it back every which way. Tom and his wife and two girls live in Austin, but they come and see me as often as they can.

"Uncle Samuel, is everything okay?"

"Believe it or not, I've got a legal question for you."

I tell him what happened. "I want to do something for Dora Lee's grandson. That shiftless Rodell will take the easiest suspect he can find, and I'm afraid it's Greg."

"First off," Tom says, "get this boy a lawyer. Is there anybody around there you feel good about hiring?" That's code for: Is there a competent lawyer in this one-horse town?

"There's one person. If I can get her to help me out."

"Why wouldn't she?"

"No need to go into it. If she won't do it, I'll have to take second-best."

"You let me know if you need anything. I'll do what I can from here." His voice is warm and I know he means it.

"Tell Vicki and the girls hi, and you all don't be strangers."

When I get off the phone, I wipe my eyes. Since Jeanne died, sometimes I feel like I don't have good sense. What I really would like is for Tom to say he'll drop everything, move down here with his family, and set up practice. I don't mean I really want that; I just mean if the world was a perfect place, he'd live down the street.

I take some time to stand and contemplate my favorite painting, a Wolf Kahn. I've got pieces that are worth more, but nothing else that calms me and somehow makes me think Jeanne is close by. After a minute, I know I'm just procrastinating, so I go back to the phone. I'm stepping off into slippery territory when I call Jenny Sandstone. It's a test of how far I'm willing to go to help this boy.

Jenny is a small-town lawyer, so she doesn't have a secretary, just an answering machine. I tell the machine that I need Jenny to call me and I leave my number.

My stomach tells me it's lunchtime, so I heat up some leftover beef stew. I'm just scraping the bottom of the bowl when the phone rings.

"You ready to give up?" Jenny's voice booms at me.

I don't take the bait. "I need to come in and talk to you when you've got time."

"I've got to go over to Bryan this afternoon, but I can spare a half hour if you can get over here now."

I put the stew dish out on the back porch for Zelda, my cat, to clean up, and head over to town.

Five minutes later I draw up in front of Jenny's office. It's on the main street, in a snappy new two-story office building that went up just before the economy hit the skids. Inside, you could think you're in a city. It's all carpet and cream-colored walls and sleek furniture.

Jenny's office is on the second floor, a nice big space for a big woman. Jenny's close to six feet tall, almost my height, with a lot of meat packed onto her. She's dressed in a bright blue suit that doesn't get on well with her red hair and white complexion. "I hope you have good news for me," she says.

"I might have. I don't know. That's not what I'm here about." I've been thinking about it on the way over, and maybe I'm ready to give her what she wants. About two years ago she bought the place next door to mine. Like mine, the house fronts onto town property, but juts back several acres. Her property isn't quite as big as mine, but it doesn't need to be. I run my cattle on mine, and she only keeps a couple of horses. It came pretty clear that she thought I'd be willing to let her horses have access to my tank—the one I had dredged and lined and stocked with fish for my own use and to water my cows.

I'll be honest; I didn't like the presumption. But the bigger problem is that I can't stand horses. A stupider animal never lived. Give me a good, solid cow any day. So I told her no, that I wanted the fence kept closed between her place and mine, and she's been on me ever since. Now she has something I want—her expertise. Theoretically, I should just be able to hire it with money. But small towns don't deal in theory.

"Let's sit down and see what's what," she says, and her smile would melt butter. I sit down and set my hat on the edge of her desk. The way she looks at it makes me see it through her eyes. It's got a good bit of wear on it, including a few stains I never paid much attention to. I move it to the seat next to me.

I tell her about Dora Lee and the boy, and I can see she's interested right away.

"This is a potential criminal case you're handing me," she says. "I don't get to try my hand at those too often."

"I'm hoping it won't come to that."

"What are you hoping will happen?"

"As I see it, we can be poised if the boy is actually arrested, to get a judge to set bail on him, then I can get him out and Rodell won't have him close to hand. Then maybe I can talk Rodell into doing some actual investigating, so he can find out who really killed Dora Lee."

"You're dreaming. Rodell wouldn't know how to investigate his way out of an outhouse with two doors."

"Somebody's going to have to figure out who killed Dora Lee, or that boy is in big trouble."

"Somebody." She smirks.

"I don't know what you have to grin about. You're supposed to be a hotshot lawyer, and it sounds like you don't care a thing about Dora Lee or her grandson."

"Whoa. Just whoa now." A pink flush is rising up her neck. "Who says I'm a hotshot lawyer?"

I groan. "I don't want to get into it with you, Jenny. If you don't want the case, say so. I'll see if Bubba Clark can do it. Or I can try to find somebody in Bobtail."

Jenny gets up and folds her arms across her ample chest. "Get off your high horse, Samuel. I didn't say I wouldn't take the case. I just want you to be realistic. Unless you find somebody to track down who killed poor Dora Lee, there's no sense in spending a dime on her grandson's case." She walks over to a small refrigerator and opens it. "You want a Coke?"

I tell her no, and she takes out a Coke and snaps the cap.

"How am I going to find somebody to figure out what happened? You know anybody?"

"You."

I rear back in my seat, and realize now what the smirk was about. "That is not going to happen, and you know it."

"I don't know it." She sits back down, lacing her hands on the desk in front of her. "The way I hear it, you're the only decent lawman this town ever had."

"The way you hear it is right, with the emphasis on the 'had.' It might have escaped your notice, but I'm a good bit over the hill."

She contemplates me for a long minute. "I'm trying to decide how much flattery you can take."

"Lay it on," I say.

"You don't look like you're that old, you don't act old, you're sharp, and my bet is you're bored to death playing with those damn cows all day. You told me yourself you were snooping around in Dora Lee's house this morning before the blood was dry. And," she points a finger at me, "you say you want to help this boy. I say there's no one else to do it. I'll go so far as to say that if you don't put your oar in, I won't get in the boat." She looks at her watch and jumps to her feet. "I've got to get out of here. Call me at home and tell me what you decide to do." She snatches up a briefcase the size of a suitcase and a shoulder bag and heads for the door.

At the door she turns around. "Lock up behind you, don't snoop around, and don't think I'm giving up on getting your permission to use your tank."

She's gone, leaving me feeling like I've been on the tail end of a tornado. *Jeanne*, I think to myself, *What in the world should I do?*

Instead of Jeanne's face popping into my head, it's Loretta's, with her pursed lips and her scolding voice. "What were you doing snooping around in Dora Lee's house? You think you can figure out what happened? You're acting like an old fool, living in the past."

My reputation as a lawman is built on an incident that happened twenty or more years ago. In my third term as police chief, I got bored and figured it was time to give it up. Jarrett Creek isn't exactly a hotbed of crime. Mostly it's arresting youngsters who've gotten drunk and rowdy after the homecoming game, or breaking up a knife fight down at the Two Dog on the outskirts of town. I was anticipating turning the reins over to somebody else and going into business with a local landman, when all hell broke loose. Somebody robbed our little state bank, shot the teller, then went over to the bank president's house and killed him. Overnight we had reporters here from Houston and San Antonio, and the town was in an uproar.

On the spot to avoid having the Jarrett Creek police look like a pack of clowns, I managed to put together a few ideas and figured out who was responsible for the mayhem. There was a little drama involved when I cornered the suspect and had to talk him out of shooting a girl he'd taken hostage. It all came out okay, but the town insisted that I go one more round as chief, which meant I missed out on the business opportunity. That worked out for the best, though, because my prospective partner had a heart attack a year later, and it turned out his affairs were in a mess.

I've been sitting in Jenny's office for twenty minutes staring at the wall, and now I pay attention to a nice little print hanging there. I wonder if she knows anything about the artist, which brings me back to Greg. Damn, I don't even know the boy's last name. So maybe that's where I should start, going over to the jail and spending a few minutes getting to know him a little better. Just because he's an artist doesn't mean he couldn't be a killer, too.

CHAPTER 3

I go on down to the Jarrett Creek city police station, figuring Rodell won't have gotten around to questioning Greg. Police headquarters is in a brick building about as big as a gas station. Besides Rodell, there are two full-time and two part-time cops. One of the full-timers, James Harley Krueger, is on duty behind the desk today. He's a short man with a stray-dog face and a personality to match. James Harley's dad is the school principal and almost as ignorant as his son. How James Harley got through police training is a mystery.

"Hey, Chief Craddock, what can I do for you?"

"Rodell around?"

His eyes go all shifty. "He's gone on an errand."

The errand Rodell has gone off on is drinking, either at the Two Dog or Carl White's place. It aggravates me that he's left that boy to collect a case of nerves and allowed Dora Lee's killer to take his sweet time getting out of town.

"Can I talk to the boy you've got in custody?"

James Harley scratches his chin. "I don't know if anybody's supposed to go in there."

I put my hands on the desk and lean over him. "James Harley, you know I was chief of police for sixteen years, don't you?"

"Yessir."

"Well, I'm here to tell you there's no law against letting a citizen have access to somebody in custody. Unless you think I'm going to break him out of jail."

"Aw, Chief Craddock, you know I don't think that." He stands up and puts his hat on, which strikes me as perverse, seeing that we're just walking into the next room. "I'll take you back there."

We walk back where two cells are located. One of them is empty. The boy is lying on a bunk in the other one. Since the building is only a few years old, you'd think it would be clean and cool. But the air-conditioning that has it about 60 degrees up front doesn't reach back here, where it feels about 85 degrees. It smells like old piss, and the walls are covered with graffiti of the kind you'd expect in a small town jail—pictures of anatomy and words to describe it. The boy sits up as soon as he sees me.

I wait for James Harley to open the cell, but he stands there, looking like a spooked cow.

"Will you open the door so I can go in there and talk to the prisoner?"

"I got to get the keys," he says and ambles off to the front.

"You doing okay?" I ask the boy.

He slaps at a mosquito on the back of his neck. He's still wearing the clothes he was painting in, and they're all covered with pastel dust. Rodell didn't even give him a chance to clean up. "I wish they'd just come and ask me what they need to ask."

James Harley comes back and lets me into the cell. I tell him I don't need him hanging around. By now he's decided I can boss him around, so he gets on back to the front office, presumably to resume his business of staring out the front window.

"We need to talk," I say, sitting down on the bunk next to Greg.

He shoves his hands under his thighs as if to keep them still. There's a film of sweat over his face and I can feel the damp collecting on my upper lip. Mosquitoes are humming all around us.

"First of all, I'm embarrassed to say I don't remember your last name."

"Marcus."

"Greg Marcus. Greg, talk to me about your family. Are your dad's folks still alive? Any aunts and uncles?"

It takes him a few seconds to get started talking. He tells me he has family down in Harlingen.

"Give me a few details."

He sighs. "My daddy's folks still live on their old place down there, but my grandma has Parkinson's, and my Aunt Patsy says she thinks they're going to have to move into town with her." He gives a little snort, the first time I've seen anything but his gloomy side.

"What's funny?"

"I don't see how that's going to work out. My aunt and uncle are real religious and have about a hundred kids, seems like. My granddad likes his whiskey, and I don't think Patsy's going to put up with that."

"You just have the one aunt?"

"On my daddy's side, yes. But I guess my mamma had a sister I never met who moved to California when she was eighteen." He's not looking at me as he recounts all this information.

"Her name is Caroline," I tell him. I haven't heard a word about her in twenty-five years. She broke Dora Lee's heart when she took off to California barely out of high school. After a while Dora Lee stopped talking about her. The important thing now is that somebody needs to find out where she is and notify her of what happened.

"Did your grandma ever tell you anything about her?"

The boy turns his head to look at me. "Only way I even knew I had an aunt was because Grandma told me a few weeks back. She said she got a letter from her." He blinks and turns his gaze back to the dingy wall opposite us.

"Well, son, don't hold out on me. What did the letter say?"

The boy shakes his head. "She didn't tell me. But I don't think she was too happy about it. She was snappish for the next couple of days after she got it."

I'm getting my comeuppance. I thought I knew a lot about Dora Lee, but she didn't tell me about the letter or about her dog dying. Seems like relying on me like she did, she would have said something about both things. I guess she had her secret side, like everybody else.

"I take it after your folks died there was never any talk about you going to live with your aunt and uncle in Harlingen."

"No, Grandma said she was glad to have me, and I'd been there so much it was like home number two."

I remember that when Greg was born, Dora Lee doted on him like he was the first and best child to ever come along.

"You and your grandma ever have words?"

He shoots a glance my way, then down at the floor. "Every now and then. But mostly we did okay."

"Any problems lately?"

He scratches the back of his neck and shifts around on the cot. "Not problems, exactly. Or I should say one problem in particular. I was thinking I ought to move to Houston so I could find me a job and take some arts classes. She didn't like the idea. I knew she'd be lonesome without me, but . . ."

"But you felt like you needed to stretch your wings."

"It wasn't like I wasn't grateful for everything she's done for me. I told her I wouldn't be that far away, and I'd come out to visit. She told me she'd think about selling if she knew where to go, but I didn't want her to do that. I love the farm."

"Speaking of that, do you know if your grandma had a will?"

He shakes his head. "She tried to bring it up once or twice, but I didn't like talking about it. Her dying, I mean. I guess I was a fool."

"Now, don't talk that way. Nobody wants to dwell on the people they love dying. It's only natural with what you went through with your folks being killed untimely, you'd be shy of thinking on it."

That's two things that need to be done—contact Caroline, and find out whether Dora Lee had a will.

Greg springs up and starts to pace, running his hands back and forth across his head. "I don't know what I'm going to do now. I sure can't keep up the farm, but I hate to let it go."

"You just hang on," I say. "Let's take your situation one step at a time. We don't know one another, but I was a good friend to your grandma. I'm going to do what I can to help you out. First thing, we've got to get you out of here. And then I think it might be good if you came to stay at my place for a few days."

He stops in front of me, stubborn written all over his face. "I don't see how I can do that. I appreciate the offer, but I've got to get back to my cabin."

I nod, knowing he's worried about his painting. "What would you think about me staying out at Dora Lee's for a few days?"

He paces to the little barred window that looks out onto the parking lot. "I don't want to put you out. I don't mind being out there by myself."

It occurs to me that he doesn't seem worried that whoever killed his grandma will come back for him. Which could mean he knows who did it. Or it could just mean he's young and doesn't think anything could happen to him. "You won't be putting me out. I consider it a favor to your grandma."

He nods. I can see he's in better shape than when I got here.

"Good, that's settled. I'm going to go looking for Rodell and see if I can't talk him into releasing you. Now be prepared. You may have to stay here tonight if I can't find Rodell. But I'll have you out tomorrow at the latest." The mosquito finally lands on my arm, and I nail him. "Meanwhile, what you can do is be thinking over the last few days. Try to remember if anything unusual happened. Even the smallest little thing."

The Two Dog is about as low a dive as you'll find. Fifteen feet outside the city limits, it looks like it was built out of rotten lumber that someone discarded after tearing down the oldest house in town, which is exactly what happened. The interior is strung with blue lights behind the bar. It has a dance floor big enough for two couples and an old-fashioned jukebox with tunes that represent the worst of fifties' and sixties' country and rock. I don't know whether Oscar can't afford to update the music or if he's just stuck in time.

When I walk in there's a version of "Mr. Sandman" playing by girls who can't carry a tune. Since the place is only about ten feet by twelve feet, with four stools and a bar the length of my kitchen table, I can see pretty quickly that Rodell isn't here. Oscar says he hasn't seen Rodell and tells me he'll let him know I'm looking for him if he comes by.

Next stop is Carl White's pasture across the tracks. Carl built a shack out there to get away from his wife. Apparently it doesn't bother her one bit that Carl goes out there most afternoons, plus he heads out to the shack first thing Saturday morning and doesn't come home until suppertime on Sunday. Sure enough when I drive down the dirt road leading to the shack, there's Rodell's police car parked alongside Carl's truck.

The two of them are sitting out behind the shack in the shade, boots propped up on a rickety old table. The table holds enough empty beer bottles to make up a case between them. I can see right away from the little hog eyes that Rodell swivels my way that he's so soused that he's probably completely forgotten about the boy.

Carl offers me a beer, and I accept it. The business I've come to discuss will go smoother if I start out being sociable. I ask Carl if he's done any fishing lately and he says he hasn't. We toss around a few ideas about the chances of the high school football team this year, conversing without the benefit of Rodell's input. He seems to be biding his time. Or maybe he's too drunk to string words together.

I test the waters: "Rodell, why in God's name have you got Dora Lee's boy locked up? You know he wouldn't hurt her."

Carl rears back and blinks at Rodell as if this is the first he's heard anything about the boy.

"I don't know nothing of the kind." Rodell enunciates his words as if they might slip away from him.

"I'll tell you what. I'd appreciate it if you'd release him to my custody. I'll see to it he stays put while you get your ducks in a row for the district attorney."

He works his mouth around a little, keeping his eyes on his bottle of beer. I expect it hadn't occurred to him that his case has to pass muster with the DA. Although the DA isn't fond of defendants, he's a stickler for details, and not a relative of Rodell's. A slow smile sneaks up on his face. "I'll let him sit in the jail for a couple of days and he might be ready to tell me the truth about what happened."

The easy way didn't work. "I hadn't wanted to tell you this," I say, "but I'm hiring Jenny Sandstone to help the boy out."

"The hell you are!"

"I am. And as soon as she gets back from Bryan today, she's going over to Bobtail and get a judge to set bail so I can pull him out of that stink house jail."

"The hell . . ."

"So you can save us some trouble and just let him out now." Rodell's head is kind of hanging down like it's too heavy for his neck. I lean my head down so I can look up at him. "What do you say?"

"I say you're an interferin' son of a bitch."

I look over at Carl to see if I can get a little support, but he's concentrating on staring off into the weeds and smoking a cigarette. I doubt he's kept up with the conversation.

"Carl, thanks for the beer. I'll be on my way. Take it easy, Rodell."

When I get back to Jenny's office it's almost four o'clock. I'm itchy because I want to be sure we have time to get a judge if it's necessary. I don't want Greg having to stay in the jail overnight. Some boys it would just roll off their backs, but I get the feeling it would be hard on him.

There's a chair down the hall outside somebody's office, so I haul it to Jenny's door and sit down. While I wait for her to show up, I finally have a minute to pay some mind to what happened to Dora Lee. And my part in it. Even though it makes me feel bad, I force myself to recall the details of our conversation last night. I don't know what time she called, but it wasn't quite dark, so I probably hadn't been asleep long. Let's call it nine thirty. She asked if she was disturbing me and I said not at all. Thinking back on it, I'm hoping I didn't sound impatient with her. I'd hate to think that the last friend she talked to would have brushed her off. Assuming I was the last person she called.

Anyway, she said, "I know you think I'm crazy, and I'm ashamed to be disturbing you for it, but whoever was spying on me a couple of weeks back is outside again. He's sitting in his car out there on the road."

"You don't have any idea who it is or what they want?"

"No, and it scares me.

"Have you seen him up close?"

"Just the car. It's a newish car, kind of fancy."

Thinking about that now, I believe that was the first time she'd described a concrete detail about a car.

"Dora Lee, can you think of any reason why someone would want to spy on you?" I said.

"Now you say that, it sounds silly. But I just have this bad feeling."

And all the time she was talking I was thinking she was just imagining things, riled up because her grandson was talking about moving to Houston so he could get a job, and she'd be by herself out there again.

Jenny Sandstone rescues me from my low moment. She comes booming down the short hallway. "Have you put any thought to what I said?"

"You don't make a lot of small talk, do you?" I say.

She unlocks the door and waves me inside. "I don't see the point. I'm busy."

We sit down and she takes her shoes off with a groan. I tell her about my talk with the boy and my idea about staying out at Dora Lee's place. "I don't want Rodell to know I'm snooping around, and that way I can do it without him knowing."

"See? That's why I want you to take charge of this investigation. Rodell never would have thought of something that slick. And there's no way in hell he'll ever catch who did this."

"I know you're right. Any chance of getting that boy out of jail tonight?"

She dials a number and asks for Judge Herrera. "It's important," she says. She tells whoever she's talking to that she'll wait and in a minute the judge comes on the phone and they talk.

I'm impressed with Jenny's combination of sweet talk and legalese. I can tell by her end of the conversation that the judge knows that Rodell is incompetent and will keep the boy in jail just for the hell of it. She tells him I'm willing to put up the bail if it comes to that. She listens a little more, then hangs up and says, "Let's get on over to the jail and spring that boy."

"What about me paying for the bail?"

"Judge Herrera said if he hasn't been arrested, we don't need bail. But there's no reason Rodell has to know that. We'll just tell him the judge is letting the boy out. Judge Herrera says he trusts you."

I've never even met the man, but a benefit of living in a sparsely populated area is that your reputation means something. I'm as good as my word, and I guess he knows it.

CHAPTER 4

Even though I know Greg is itching to get back home, I tell him I have to do a couple of things at my place before we go out to Dora Lee's. I need to pack my clothes and call Truly Bennett and ask him if he'll keep an eye on my cows while I'm gone. You have to check on cows often in high summer, because they can get themselves into the damnedest trouble with boggy ground or rattlesnakes. But I also have another reason for wanting to get Greg to my house.

When we pull up in front, he tells me he'll stay in the car, but I insist on him coming in. "It's too hot out here. You'll fry."

I walk ahead of him across the porch and in the front door, then turn to see his reaction when he walks in. At first, it doesn't register, but then I see him freeze and slowly take in the art I have hung on my walls. Like he's in a trance, he walks over to the little Bischoff figure drawing, then to the Thiebaud, which has pride of place above the fireplace. Then he moves on around the room. He takes a long time, like a parched man drinking water. He moves from one painting to another, not saying a word. When he turns to me, it's like he's seeing me with new eyes. "These are real, aren't they?"

"Yes, they are."

He takes another turn around the room. "Who would have known?" His voice is quiet, as if he's talking to himself, but then his gaze comes back to me. "I hardly ever got to see anything like this except in books. My folks took me to Houston a few times to some museums, but that's all. I didn't think anybody around here knew anything about art."

"We're a scarce breed; that's a fact." I tell him about Jeanne and how we got interested in art and started buying a painting here and there and having a fine time doing it. "Most people who walk in here don't even see the paintings. Come on back here."

I show him the art in the bedroom and then the dining room, which I hardly ever use since Jeanne died. We put the few sculptures we bought there, one a Manuel Neri that we bought early on. There's no way I could afford most of these things nowadays.

"This art is from a good ways back. It must be worth a lot. Don't you worry about somebody coming in here and stealing something?" he says.

"Not too many people understand what's here. And it's well insured." I leave him to soak it in while I go pack a few things. It makes me feel good to have someone in here who can appreciate the art. Anyone who notices it at all usually says some version of "I don't get all these scribbles and shapes. I like things to look like what they are." Every couple of years, we used to get a little herd of people from Houston who took a tour of private collections. But last year, with Jeanne not here to show them around, I begged off.

On the way out to Dora Lee's place, I ask Greg how he came to know he could be an artist. "My daddy liked to paint and he used to let me paint with him. I took to it right off, and he liked that. He's the one who started bringing me art books."

I glance over at the boy and ask straight out. "He didn't mind that you have more talent than he did?"

"He said for him it was just a hobby, something he liked. He said I had a gift and not to let it get away from me." He turns his face away to look out the side window.

We're quiet the rest of the way out to the farm. I'm thinking about the work I saw in his cabin, wondering how he learned as much as he has. We park at Dora Lee's, neither of us is in a hurry to get out of the truck. It's dusk and there's already a look of gloom about Dora Lee's farm. Her big vegetable garden looks dry and droopy, like it has been deserted for a lot longer than a day.

We finally climb out of the pickup, and out of habit head around back to the kitchen door. We're almost there before I realize it's a mistake. Luckily, the door has been locked and Greg has to search out his keys. That way I make it to the door before he can open it. There are two reasons I don't want him to go inside. One, they won't have cleaned up after they took Dora Lee away, and I don't want him to be faced with the aftermath. And two, I want to see the scene with fresh eyes. This morning I was so shocked, that I might have missed something. With so many people milling around in the kitchen, the crime scene won't be worth much, but I want to get a better sense of it.

I tell him to go on and get settled in his place. "I'll call you when I have something fixed for us to eat." He doesn't need to be asked twice, just shoots off, itching to get to his cabin.

I set my bag down inside the kitchen and stand looking around. The crime scene tape is wadded up and thrown on the floor. I see a bloody smear from a shoe that I'm sure wasn't there this morning. I wonder if Rodell even tried to preserve the integrity of the scene.

Most of Dora Lee's blood was caught by her clothes, very little of it spilling onto the floor. Some is spattered on one cabinet, so I know her killer attacked while she stood with her back to the sink.

The thing is, I see no sign that she might have known what was coming. If she'd been scared, there would likely be something out of place. She might have tried to run and maybe would have shoved a chair aside, or maybe would have thrown something at her killer and that would be lying on the floor. But there's nothing like that. Of course somebody moved two kitchen chairs this morning to hold the crime scene tape, so I guess I'll never know if they were out of place when the law got here.

I also took note this morning that there weren't any wounds on her hands from trying to fend off her attacker. Whoever did this was talking to her and he walked up and stuck the knife in before she had a chance to react. It wasn't a stranger came in here. It was somebody she knew. I think about Greg. I don't want my regard for his talent to blind me to reality. I have to consider the possibility that he had a problem with Dora Lee that he's not talking about, that led him to simmer and then finally snap.

I walk into the front room and pull the curtain aside. I can see the road from here. If a woman was afraid somebody was out there, she might come in here several times in an evening to look out. I bring a lamp closer to the curtains, and sure enough there are smudges where her hand moved the curtain aside.

I wait for a car to pass to find out if I can hear it from where I'm standing. It's about five minutes before someone passes, speeding fast down the road. Sound travels well over the bare field from the road to the house, and it's easy to hear the car, even with the windows shut and the air-conditioning running. But how did Dora Lee know it was a "fancy car?" And then it strikes me. She didn't say passing by, she said, "somebody out on the road." I wonder if the car stopped out there and sat for a while and she saw it. The idea chills me.

I sink into my familiar chair across from the one Dora Lee always sat in to work. Her sewing bag is next to her chair with a quilted square she was stitching laid carefully across the top. For months after Jeanne died, I used to come out here often and sit with Dora Lee. She was always working on a quilt and I'd watch her, not really seeing her, just numb, glad to be with someone who was familiar with every phase of Jeanne's decline. Sometimes we'd have the TV on, but often Dora Lee would sing while she worked. She had a sweet, clear singing voice and seemed to know the words to every song, from show tunes to old-time hymns. And sometimes she just talked about everyday things, and I'd let her words bind themselves around me.

As I sit here I'm remembering Dora Lee telling me something about an art teacher Greg had in high school, but the details escape me. I feel like rusty parts of my brain are trying to fire up, like a jalopy that's been sitting in the elements and needs some grease. I wish I'd paid more attention.

Back in the kitchen, I get to the task of cleaning up the blood. The kitchen floor is linoleum, so it cleans up pretty easy. The cabinets are a little more problematic, but elbow grease prevails. While I clean, my memory comes clearer in fits and starts. There was an art teacher at the high school in Bobtail who took an interest in Greg and gave him lessons after school. Dora Lee complained because she thought the teacher had meant he would teach Greg for free and came to find out he wanted to be paid more than she thought it was worth. "He's got mighty big ideas for a small-town teacher," she said. Even after Greg got out of high school the lessons continued, but a few months ago there was a falling out of some kind, and the lessons stopped. Dora Lee said she never liked the man.

I rummage around in the refrigerator and find some leftover chicken that smells all right, and I open a can of peas. I figure that will be enough for tonight. It occurs to me we could have eaten in town, but I don't feel like going back in. One thing for sure, we're not going to eat in the kitchen.

When Greg comes in for dinner, his eyes go straight to the place where his grandmother was lying. He crosses his arms across his chest, shoving his hands into his armpits as if he's cold. "I just can't believe she's gone."

"You've lost too many for as young as you are," I say. "You'll just have to take it slow. Come on in here and eat."

He looks surprised, but follows me into the living room, where the dining table is pushed up against the wall. I've cleared off the lace cloth and the bric-a-brac and set us a couple of plates. He nods, understanding that I decided we didn't need to eat in the room where Dora Lee died.

"It's not much of a meal, but it'll do," I say.

He has the appetite of youth, and digs in. I wait until we've eaten a little before I ask him my question about the dishes.

"It was my job to wash, and she'd dry them and put them away."

"Did she usually wait to do that?"

"No, she'd dry while I washed. She said it was a good way to end the day, doing a task together like that." He puts his fork down and pushes his plate away.

"So why didn't she dry them last night?"

His eyes stray to the front window. "I had just started washing the dishes when she came out here into the front room. I asked her where she was going, and she said she wanted to check and make sure nobody was outside." He looks back at me.

"Did you think that was odd?"

He shakes his head. "I didn't think much about it either way. I was in hurry to get back out to my place, so I just told her I was done with the dishes, and I was going back." His voice is so quiet I can barely hear him. "I guess I should have paid more attention, though."

"We've all got our burden about that," I say. And then I confess to him about his grandma's phone call to me last night. I hadn't planned on telling him, but I want him to understand he's not the only one to dismiss her fears. "My question to you is, can you think of anything unusual that happened in the last couple of weeks? Anybody call, or come by here? Or did she go somewhere she usually didn't go?"

His mouth drops open. "She did go somewhere! She went to Houston!"

"When was this?"

"Two, three weeks ago, I don't remember exactly."

"But it couldn't have been all that unusual for her to go to Houston."

He scowls. "That's true. The difference was, usually she took me with her, 'cause she was worried about driving that far alone. But this time she just asked me if she could bring me anything from the art supply store."

"Did you ask her if you could go?"

He blinks at me a couple of times, thinking. "I did, but she said she needed to go by herself. The thing is, she seemed kind of excited, like she

42

had a secret mission. I was pretty annoyed because I would like to have gone with her to pick out some supplies." He shakes his head, his mouth grim. "And to top it off, she forgot to get the stuff I asked her to bring."

"She forgot? That doesn't sound like Dora Lee."

"I couldn't believe it! I asked her why she'd bothered to ask me for a list if she wasn't going to get it for me."

"What did she have to say about that?"

"She said she was sorry, that she had something on her mind." He frowns. "And I didn't ask her what it was because I was so mad." His leg is jittering and he's frowning so hard that I figure he's holding something back.

"I expect the argument didn't end there."

He shakes his head. "We had words. I said I was ready to move out right away, that I was sick and tired of having to depend on her."

"She probably got upset about that."

His face is bright red and his eyes snap fire at me. "I had been telling her I needed to move on. Her forgetting my supplies was kind of the last straw."

"It lit a fire under your tail."

"That's right! I'd figured out that if I was going to ever get out of here, it might as well be sooner rather than later."

"You think Dora Lee had the money to send you to school, but she held out because she didn't want you to leave?"

Greg is suddenly still, as if he understands the drift of my questions, that I'm trying to find out just how desperate he was to get to art school. "Sometimes I thought so, but if you think I killed my grandma so I could get her money, you're wrong."

He gets up and starts stacking the dishes, clattering them in his anger.

"Sit down, son. I'm not accusing you of anything, but I need to know exactly what went on between the two of you. Some folks will be quick to accuse you, and the best way I can help you is if I know all the facts."

He eases back down, but keeps a wary eye out. "What else do you want to know?"

"Dora Lee paid for lessons for you a while back."

He sneers. "For what they were worth."

"You didn't think much of your teacher?"

He shrugs. "He thought he was a lot better painter than he was. He bragged that one day he would make it big time as an artist. Any fool could see he didn't do anything but paint pictures of cactus and bluebonnets."

"He taught you some things though. You have some basics under your belt."

"Sure he taught me some basics. But I outgrew him."

I'd met a few artists over the years when Jeanne and I were buying art, and I had seen Greg's arrogance before. I wonder if a person has to have a bit of that cocksure streak to get anywhere as an artist. But it had to be hard on a teacher who nurtured a kid, when he turned his back on you.

Greg stands up again and picks up a handful of dishes. "Besides, Grandma said he charged too much."

I help him carry the things into the kitchen. "Do you think that's why she wanted you to stop taking lessons?" I say to his back.

He puts the dishes in the sink and turns, cocking an eyebrow. "She never liked Mr. Eubanks. She thought he put ideas into my head. I told her I had enough ideas on my own and didn't need somebody like him to tell me what I could do."

"If she had been able to continue paying for lessons, would you have wanted to keep on?"

He shrugs. "I guess, but it didn't matter much to me. It was a big deal to him, though. He came out here and pitched a fit with her." He hooks his thumbs in his pants and looks down at the floor, shaking his head. "She didn't take a thing off of him. He left with his tail between his legs."

He looks up, his eyes wet with the memory and we smile at each other, remembering how Dora Lee could get her feathers ruffled.

I've still got work to do this evening, so I send Greg to his cabin, telling him that I'll wash up tonight, but that after this it's his job again.

The whole time while I wash the dishes, I'm trying to think what Dora Lee was up to in Houston. Naturally, my thoughts go to M. D. Anderson, the big cancer hospital where Jeanne and I spent too much of our time the last year of her life. I wonder if Dora Lee had something wrong, and she wasn't telling anyone. But Greg said she seemed excited, which doesn't sound like somebody facing bad health.

Which brings me to what I've got to do tonight. I'm awfully tired, but I know tomorrow is going to be full of chaos. People will be calling and bringing food and dropping by to nose around. There will be funeral arrangements to make and people to contact. So if I'm going to have a quiet time to poke around for clues as to what might have happened to Dora Lee, it will have to be tonight.

My knee is throbbing from a day of unaccustomed activity, so I swallow a couple of Tylenol, make myself a cup of coffee, and tackle Dora Lee's spare room. She kept her business correspondence in a massive rolltop desk that's so battered it looks like someone used a baseball bat on it. Her laptop computer is shoved to the back of the desk. I expect she used it about as much as I do mine, which is hardly at all, so I'll look at it later. I feel funny messing with her papers, but I finally settle in and get down to work.

I sort the papers into a pile for bills, another for business correspondence, one for personal letters, and still another for ads and notices. I suppose I could throw the last pile away, but for now it's best to keep it all. I learned that the hard way after Jeanne died, when I threw away something that looked like an ad but turned out to be a stock certificate. You haven't lived until you go through a week's worth of garbage looking for one thin piece of paper.

Another stack is for business cards, which Dora Lee collected in abundance, and another for bank statements. I have resolved not to read the contents of any of the pieces of paper. It's better to get it all sorted first. But on a bank statement from last month, my eye falls on the balance, $2,600. I have a couple different accounts myself, keeping only a small balance in the one for everyday expenses. I replenish it when it gets low. I expect Dora Lee did the same thing.

It takes me until almost eleven o'clock before I've emptied the drawers, an accordion file, and all the little cubbyholes of the desk. It pleases me that I don't find any bills or correspondence from M. D. Anderson. So she didn't have cancer. Then I realize how silly it is to think that. Either way, she's gone.

I expected to find three things that are nowhere to be seen. I haven't located a will. And I haven't seen the letter Greg said came from Dora Lee's daughter Caroline. But the most worrisome is that I haven't found statements from any other bank, nor evidence that she had any other funds. No stocks or bonds, no savings accounts, and no CDs. It makes my blood run cold to think that Dora Lee was down to $2,600.

By midnight I have scoured her papers, and it's clear she was barely solvent. The only money she had coming in on a regular basis besides her social security was a pittance she got for renting her pasture out. And that ended early in the summer when the man renting it sold out his herd and moved to be near his daughter. Besides that, she sold the occasional quilt, but that didn't amount to much.

I found the deed to her place in a drawer at her bedside, and apparently before Teague died he mortgaged it to the hilt. She's paid down the mortgage over the years, but it has broken her back to do it. I'm ashamed that I never thought twice about her financial security, as lucky as I've been on that score.

It was only after I married Jeanne that I realized her family had more money than they let on. Not by big city standards, but for someone growing up in a small town as I did, it seemed like a lot. She had a nice little trust fund from her grandparents, and when her younger brother died with no family, he left us another chunk. If we'd had to depend on my salary as chief of police and then as an oil and gas landman, there's no way we could have been able to buy the pieces of art that we were so partial to.

And here is evidence that my friend Dora Lee could have used a hand. Not that she would have accepted me giving her money, but I could have made her life easier by arranging a loan to be paid back "someday."

I have one more task to complete before I can quit. I go looking for Dora Lee's purse and find it stowed on a side counter of the kitchen near the telephone. Sure enough, like every woman I've ever known, Dora Lee kept a tiny little address book. Like Jeanne's, it's dog-eared and worn, filled in with tiny print and crossings out that make it practically illegible. But I manage to put together a list of people I need to call to let them know what happened. And I wonder if someone on this list is the person who decided to end Dora Lee's life.

CHAPTER 5

I had wondered if I could stand to sleep in Dora Lee's bed, but there's no good alternative. The single bed in the room she used as an office is piled high with quilting gear, and I don't have the energy to move it.

I'm normally an early riser, but when the phone rings the next morning, it wakes me up and I see that I've slept until eight o'clock. I know before I answer the phone that it's Loretta, acting as if nothing unhappy passed between us yesterday.

"How did you know I was out here?" I ask.

"I went by your place to drop off some cinnamon buns and Truly was just leaving. He'd been there to see to your cows and said you were going to be out at Dora Lee's."

"I guess it's all over town that I sprung Dora Lee's grandson out of jail."

"Rodell is fit to be tied, but since you had that Jenny Sandstone with you, he couldn't do anything about it."

I tell Loretta I could use help if she has the time. She can't get off the phone fast enough. I figure I have just about enough time to take a shower before she gets here.

Sure enough, I've just wiped the shaving cream off my face when I hear Loretta yoo-hooing at the back door. She has brought a plate of fresh-made cinnamon rolls that are still hot.

"You want me to knock on that boy's door and tell him there's rolls?"

She doesn't really want to, or she'd have just gone on and done it. Loretta is a generous soul, so if she has feelings against the boy, that means many others will take against him in town. I'll have to go to work on that.

I tell her to let him be. If he's asleep, he needs the rest, and if he's awake, he's probably painting, trying to make up for lost time. He's too young to know that never happens.

By the time I finish a couple of Loretta's cinnamon buns and a pot of coffee, I'm ready to get to the business of the day, and not a minute too soon. Two ladies have already shown up with casseroles and curiosity. It's going to be an asset to have Loretta here. She gives them enough information to satisfy them, and yet manages to whisk them out the door in just a few minutes.

Pretty soon I see the Baptist minister, Howard Duckworth, coming up the back steps. Duckworth is about the least godly man I ever knew. When he's not strutting himself in church, he's got a foul temper and a foul mouth and can't keep his hands off any female in his congregation under forty. I've made it my business not to be in the same room with him any longer than I have to for fear I'll say something I'll regret. I'm not religious. If the Baptists want to pay Duckworth to tell them what's right and wrong, it's their business. I happen to know that Dora Lee was part of a church group that was planning to run him out on a rail. The very idea that he will speak at her funeral irritates the hell out of me.

I leave Loretta to handle him, telling her I've got telephone calls to make. I sequester myself in Dora Lee's office. The first thing is to find out when the county will release her body so we can plan the funeral. When I reach the county morgue, they tell me that because Dora Lee was murdered her autopsy went to the head of the list and is being conducted even as we speak. The body should be ready to release by late this afternoon. Today is Friday, which means the earliest the funeral could be is Sunday afternoon, which I doubt will sit well with the Baptists. I say I'd like to talk to whoever is doing the examination of the murder weapon. The woman asks me who I am, and I tell her I'm working with Rodell. She's satisfied with that lie, because she doesn't really care who I am, as long as she gets an answer. She says she'll have the investigator get back to me.

When I call over to Landau's Funeral Home, I'm lucky to find Earnest Landau in. He took care of Jeanne's funeral and I'm grateful to have him to handle Dora Lee's. He asks me if I want to come down and pick out a casket and I tell him I can't make that decision without a member of the family, but would he start whatever groundwork is necessary so he'll be ready once I roust out Greg. He says leave it to him, and I know he means it.

Then it's time to start calling Dora Lee's relatives. This is a whole lot different from when I had to do it for Jeanne. Then I was so full of grief and anger I could barely choke out the words. As soon as Tom heard the news about Jeanne, he dropped everything and he and Vicki came down and took over.

With Dora Lee, my sorrow is tempered by a sense of outrage that's beginning to fester in me. Jarrett County is my territory, and I don't like somebody thinking they can get away with killing a good woman I've known my whole life.

You have to observe a ritual when notifying next of kin about a death. People get put out if one is called before the other, or if one gets told something that another doesn't get told. It's a delicate business. Dora Lee's living daughter, Caroline, ought to be the first person I contact. In Dora Lee's dog-eared address book, I find Caroline's number in California, but it has been crossed out and nothing written in its place. Then I remember the letter Greg said Dora Lee got from her. Maybe because it's morning and I've got some of my wits back, it occurs to me that the letter might be stashed in Dora Lee's purse, a woman's repository of all significant things.

The letter is there, the paper soft from being handled so much. It's dated July 1, six weeks ago. I figure Dora Lee wouldn't mind if I read it.

Dear Mother,

I'm writing to tell you that I'm moving to Houston. The company I'm with, Dellams Software, has decided to relocate there from Los Angeles. I wasn't happy about it at first, but have made my peace with it. In some ways I guess it will be good to get back to Texas.

I will call you when my house is set up. Maybe we can arrange to meet.

Caroline

I don't like the letter. There's no warmth to it. Caroline could be writing to a business acquaintance. She says, "maybe we can arrange to meet." Not that she'll invite Dora Lee to her house. Not that's she's looking forward to seeing her. Just that cold, begrudging statement.

Then I think I'm being mean. Caroline could have moved back and not let Dora Lee know. At least she wasn't that callous. The fact that the letter has been unfolded and refolded tells me all I need to know about how it affected Dora Lee. I hope she didn't notice the slight. I hope she died in the warmth of knowing her daughter was coming back to her. I can be such a sentimental old fool.

I still don't have a number to reach Caroline. Information in Houston doesn't have anyone by the name Caroline Parjeter. So then I get the number for Dellams Software in Houston, and ask for Caroline and am put on hold. After a while a slick-voiced young man comes on and asks who I am. I tell him I'm trying to reach Caroline because there has been a death in the family.

"I'm so sorry to hear that," he says. "But Miss Parjeter was with our California office, and she's no longer with the company."

"I see. Can you tell me if she left a way to get in touch with her?"

"If she did, all those records would be in back files."

"Back files?"

"Yes sir, we only keep employee information for a year, and Miss Parjeter hasn't worked for Dellams for two years."

I hang up and sit staring at the place where the missing picture used to hang. So there was a lie in the letter Caroline wrote to Dora Lee. She didn't transfer with Dellams—hasn't worked for them for two years. So where is she working, and how long has she been back in Texas? When Dora Lee went to Houston a couple of weeks ago, all excited, I'm wondering if she was going to visit Caroline. If so, how come she didn't tell anyone?

I go through Dora Lee's purse, carefully this time, but find nothing that would tell me where Caroline might live in Houston. Just to be sure, I call the number that was crossed out in Los Angeles. But the woman who answers says she's had the number for over a year and doesn't know any Caroline Parjeter.

In the kitchen I can hear Duckworth and Loretta jawing on and on, so I sneak out through the front door and go out to Dora Lee's car. It's a burgundy Ford Taurus, about five years old. It's clean as the day she bought it, except for a couple of business cards in the front tray. One of them is from a place called Houston Antiques 'N Art. Is it possible that Caroline has gone to work there?

I take the card back in and call the shop.

"Parjeter?" the man says. "That's an unusual name. Did she say she worked here?"

"No, I found your card and was trying to put two and two together. I guess I came up with something other than four."

"Well I never heard of her."

"Let me ask you this. Did a woman by the name of Dora Lee Parjeter come to your shop maybe two weeks ago?"

"If she did, she didn't introduce herself. Like I said, that's an unusual name and I would have remembered it."

My last resort is to go through Dora Lee's phone bills to see if I can come up with a number. I find the bills from the past few months, but they contain nothing but local calls. If Dora Lee talked to Caroline, it was an incoming call.

I've put way too much time into finding Caroline. There are other relatives to notify. Dora Lee had a sister several years younger who moved to Virginia a long time ago. I call her and she's upset, but says there's no way she can make it back for the funeral. She gets the name of the funeral home and says she'll send some flowers. Dora Lee has some distant cousins around the county, and I call one of them and ask her to notify the others. She's a practical woman, who says she'll wait until she knows exactly when the funeral will be, then make the calls.

Greg's aunt on his dad's side, Patsy Raymond, lives way down in Harlingen, so I figure I'd better let her know pretty quickly, so if she and her family want to come for the funeral they'll be able to arrange the trip.

"This is Patsy. Praise the Lord. How can I help you?" There's a TV blaring in the background and I can hear someone say, "Who is it?"

"Patsy, you don't know me, but I'm a friend of Dora Lee Parjeter."

"Hold on a minute, please. Mamma, it's a friend of Dora Lee's. Now let me talk. Sorry about that. How's Dora Lee?"

"I'm afraid I have some bad news. Dora Lee was found dead yesterday."

"Oh, but that's not bad news! That's good news. She's with Jesus! What could be better than that?"

I can think of a few things that would be better, but I don't think Patsy's up for a serious discussion. "Well, I thought you'd want to know. I think the funeral will be Sunday."

"Please don't tell me that. My family will want to be there and we don't travel on the Lord's day."

"I see. Well, it's not decided yet. I'm sure Monday will work as well. I'll call you back when I know for sure."

"How's my nephew holding up? Is he there? Can I talk to him?"

I tell her that Greg is off on an errand, but that I'll have him get in touch. I can't wait to get off the phone. I think what a nightmare it would have been for a kid who wanted to concentrate on his art to be thrown into the care of someone like Patsy.

It's time to roust Greg. I'm just rounding the corner to his cabin when Reverend Duckworth comes down the back steps. I shake his sweaty hand and he oozes platitudes on me. Thankfully, I hear the phone ring inside and Loretta calling out to me.

Loretta opens the back door. "Where have you got to? Somebody's on the phone asking for you."

"Who is it?" I climb the porch stairs with a hitch in my step. After being up so late last night, my knee is giving me fits.

"I don't recognize the voice. It's a man."

I go into the spare room to take the call.

"Samuel? This is Johnny Taylor over at the county morgue."

"Johnny, I thought you'd be long retired."

"They can't get me off the horse," he says. He laughs. I've always wondered how somebody who works with dead bodies all the time can be so cheerful. "I'm just part-time here now. My girl told me you were working with Rodell. What's that all about?"

"It was a bald-faced lie," I tell him. He laughs again. I've known him since I was chief of police. He knows exactly what Rodell is like. "I'm just nosy. Dora Lee was a friend of mine. I'm trying to get some idea of what happened here."

"Well, you're not going to get it from the knife. Whoever put that knife in her had gloves on. In August. I'm sure you know that means he planned in advance what he was going to do."

"It might have been easier if you could have told me something different," I say.

"I hear that. I'll get the report to the police by Monday, but if you have any more questions, you let me know."

I'm not all that upset by his news. Fingerprinting gets uneven results. It's probably better now, but when I was a lawman, a lot of prints never made it onto the state files. Even if they'd found prints all over the knife, whoever killed Dora Lee would have to have fingerprints on file with the state for a match to come up. Furthermore, it would have been be up to Rodell to try to pursue that lead. Now it's a moot point.

One more person that needs to be notified right away about Dora Lee is her brother-in-law, Leslie Parjeter. Dora Lee didn't care much for Leslie, telling me he was so stingy that the only Christmas present he ever let his wife buy for her girls when they were little was a bag of tiny, bitter oranges. When they got older, even that stopped.

He's got one of those high-pitched voices common to old men who have spent their lives farming and don't get much chance to exercise their vocal chords. "You say Dora Lee died?"

"That's right. Happened yesterday."

"Did she have a heart attack, or what?"

"Leslie, I'm sorry to tell you this, but somebody killed her."

"Killed her! Do they know who done it?"

"Not yet."

"Probably some young 'uns looking for money for drugs. On the television, they say kids get up to that a lot these days."

"Could be. Anyway, we're thinking about the funeral for Monday. Will you be able to make it?"

"I don't think so. I'm seventy-five years old and a little stove up, and I don't know if I can spare the money to make the trip. I'll get over there if I can."

"Where do you live?"

"I'm over here in Dimebox. I live at the old place where Teague and me grew up. Listen here, I need to ask you a question. What's your interest in this?"

It's a blunt question, but I don't take offense. All my life I've known people like Leslie who don't know much about the social niceties, but don't mean anything by their manner. "I'm an old friend of Dora Lee's. Known her my whole life, grew up with her. I knew your brother, too."

"Yep. Well, Teague was a ring-tailed tooter. We didn't get along too well, but I liked Dora Lee. She leave a will?"

"I'm not sure about that. I'm looking into it. Did you have a reason for asking?" Maybe he knows something I don't.

"I have my reasons. But also I was thinking about Dora Lee's grandson. If he's got no place to go, I could take him in. I could use a hand around the place. We couldn't pay him, like, but he'd get his three squares and someplace to put his head at night."

I can imagine what this old man means by "three squares," grits in the morning, and cornbread, beans, and greens the other two meals. "That's real generous of you, but I wouldn't count on it. I think the boy's got some plans."

"Plans. Well, I guess so. I expect he's graduated high school now. That's when the boys get their ideas. Goin' to the city and that kind of thing."

I tell him I'll have Greg call him and hang up. It starts me thinking about how people like Leslie have their whole world right where they were born. I guess I'm the same; never had a lot of desire to go anywhere else. I wouldn't live any other place on earth than Jarrett County, and I've seen a few places. After I got out of the air force, I swore I would come back to this area and you couldn't pry me out. I've stuck to it.

But at least my world opened up when I found Jeanne. Without her I could just have easily lived in a world only slightly bigger than Leslie Parjeter's.

When I go back into the kitchen, I find several people have been here to visit and are ready to leave. I exchange a few words with them, a couple of them eyeing me in an odd way, wondering how I come to be here. I slip out back to get Greg. He needs to have a presence with these folks.

CHAPTER 6

I see right off that Greg is not a person well suited to the morning. He comes to the door with his hair sticking out all over and his eyes unfocused. He smells like he slept in his clothes. When I tell him people are here to pay their respects and he ought to be there, he gives an ornery grunt and tells me he'll be over at the house after a while.

"I've let you sleep as long as I can. This is something you have to put yourself out for."

"I told you I'll be there in a minute," he says. Yesterday the shock of Dora Lee's death had him a little cowed, but today he's back to his prickly self.

I look him up and down. "It might be a good idea if you took a shower, too."

Back in the kitchen, Loretta is stowing another dish of macaroni and cheese in the refrigerator. A woman I don't recognize is sitting at the kitchen table. She introduces herself as Frances Underwood, from the next farm down. She's in her forties and skinny, all sharp edges and bright eyes with some calculation in them.

Although I've run into most people around here one time and another, I don't know the Underwoods. Dora Lee said they were a little snobbish. I sit down across the kitchen table from her. "You're the woman who found Dora Lee?"

"I am. I don't ever want something like that to happen to me again."

"It must have been terrible." I'm thinking it was a damn sight worse for Dora Lee. "What time of the morning was it?"

"Early. I was bringing Dora Lee some eggs. I've got a few good layers and she said she wouldn't mind having some fresh eggs."

"You can't find good fresh eggs like that at the grocery store," Loretta says. "How much do you get for them?"

I translate. Loretta wants to know if this woman was giving the eggs, or selling them.

"They're real reasonable. I don't charge a bit more than you'd pay at the Quick Stop."

"You can't do any better than that," Loretta says, patting the curls at the back of her neck.

"When you came to bring the eggs yesterday morning, I don't suppose you saw anybody around that shouldn't be here?" I say.

"There's nobody out and about that time of day. I like to get my business out of the way early." She has one of Loretta's cinnamon rolls in front of her and she picks off a little corner of it. "They say it was that grandson of hers that killed her."

"You ever see any signs of problems between them?" I ask.

She puts the morsel of roll into her mouth and mashes it around. She's so skinny that you just know she and food are not on good terms. "I never saw the boy more than once or twice, so I couldn't tell you."

"How long have you lived out here?"

"When Mamma had to go into a home, we moved into her house. We've been here almost two years now."

I prick up my ears. Most people around these parts move back to their parents' old place when the old people can't do for themselves. They move back to help out, not to displace them. "Wait a minute, I remember your folks. Ed and Agatha Shockley. Ed died, what is it, fifteen years ago now?"

"That's right. Mamma wore herself out with the farm after that."

"And how's your mamma doing?" Loretta saves me from having to ask. Her voice is full of sugar. She's thinking the same thing I am, that this woman stashed her old mother somewhere and confiscated her house.

"She died a few months back," Mrs. Underwood says. "Mamma

was glad we wanted to keep the old place. So many folks don't appreciate the land. But my husband wanted to do a little farming."

She wants us to know that she had her mother's blessing. But I didn't notice a lot of farming going on at the Underwoods'. Like Dora Lee's land, it is sorely depleted by years of cotton crops, and most people don't have the money to repair the soil. Alfalfa is about the only thing that will grow, and there's plenty of that, so the prices aren't worth planting it to sell.

"Let me ask you something," I say. "I was talking to Dora Lee a couple of days ago, and she said she saw a car around here that she didn't recognize. You see anything like that?"

She manages to swallow the piece of roll. "I wouldn't have noticed such a thing. My husband and I lived in San Antonio for twenty years before we came out here. We got used to seeing all kinds of people coming and going."

"What sort of work did your husband do in San Antonio?" Loretta asks.

"Wasn't just my husband. We had ourselves a real estate office. I worked right alongside him."

About then Greg comes in the back door, smelling of soap and with his hair slicked down. Mrs. Underwood's eyes widen, like she can't believe he's walking around free. And it isn't long before she scoots out of there.

Loretta fusses over the boy, and he is properly appreciative of the cinnamon rolls. By the time he wolfs down the third one, there's no way Loretta believes he could have killed his grandmother.

After that, things speed up. We have funeral arrangements to make and people in town to call. All this recalls bad memories for me, but I remind myself this boy has been through more than I've ever had to deal with, so I push it all back.

At some point I call Gary Dellmore down at the bank and tell him to set up a temporary account in my name to pay for Dora Lee's funeral and farm expenses. I tell him I'll drop by in a while to transfer some funds into it from my bank in Bobtail. He asks me why I would take care of Dora Lee's expenses. I come close to telling him it's none of his business, but if I do, it'll be all over town that Dora Lee and I were up to something. So I tell him that Dora Lee's poor grandson has nobody to fend for him and that as Dora Lee's old friend, I'm lending a hand. I tell him I'll get my money paid back when the estate is settled.

"I wouldn't count on that. Dora Lee's got it mortgaged to the limit."

I tell him there may be some things he doesn't know about. I don't mean anything by that, but it satisfies me to know that he's eaten up with curiosity. Plus, it doesn't sit well with me that he'd blab Dora Lee's financial information so easily, which is why I've always kept most of my funds in a bank in Bobtail, so Dellmore has no idea what I'm worth.

Ever since Frances Underwood introduced herself, I've been trying to remember where I saw the name Underwood recently. It has to have been in the papers I sifted through last night. It doesn't take me long to find what I'm looking for. In the stack of correspondence I put together last night, there's a letter dated last May, from Clyde Underwood. I read it over, and it makes me so mad I have to sit quiet for a minute. It seemed that Mr. Clyde Underwood wanted to do Dora Lee the favor of buying her land. Cheap.

Back when I was in my forties, after I was finished with my stint as chief of police, my brother-in-law hired me as a landman for his oil and gas exploration business. Landmen are in demand in Texas because so many folks want to find out if they have oil or gas on their property that's worth drilling for. When he first offered me the job, I said, "DeWitt, I don't know a thing about being a landman."

He said, "Samuel, you've got the first part down. You know this part of the state like the back of your hand. And the specifics of oil and gas I can teach you in a week."

And he was right. He was a shrewd businessman with a nose for oil and gas, and he said I was a quick study. I made a good living at it until I retired when Jeanne got sick. In the process I learned a good deal about what land was worth in the county—farm and ranch land, agricultural land and commercial enterprises, in addition to natural resources. What Clyde Underwood offered Dora Lee you wouldn't offer for swampland.

I sit back and put my feet up on the desk and consider if Clyde Underwood knew about Dora Lee's precarious financial situation. If I hadn't just talked to Gary Dellmore, I might not have put it together, but something tells me that Clyde had an inside track on who was hurting for money around here. And that inside track had to come from the person who held the mortgage on Dora Lee's place. That man is Gary Dellmore. I wonder what Underwood really wants with the land. There's never been an oil or gas find right around here.

I'm thinking myself into a fine temper, when I hear a car engine approaching the house. I step into the front room and see Rodell come wheeling up into the side yard, skewing the car to a stop. I go out to meet him, hoping I can head him off of Greg's trail.

Rodell untangles himself from his black Chevrolet and eyes me up and down. I can smell the alcohol leeching out of his pores. His eyes are bloodshot. "You've got yourself all set up out here, ain't you?"

"Let's cut to the chase, Rodell. What is it you're after?"

"I'm here to let you know I got a call from a Mr. Leslie Parjeter. He wanted to know what kind of a person you were, and what business you had nosing around Dora Lee's place. He said you took it upon yourself to inform him of Dora Lee's murder."

"Uh, huh. And you told him what?"

"I told him I'd come out here and check things out."

"Is that a fact? Well, now you've checked things out, how about if you tell Mr. Parjeter that everything's fine."

"I can't do that, Samuel. You're harboring the criminal that most likely killed poor Dora Lee. For all I know the two of you have cooked up to kill her and take over her property."

I'd laugh if I didn't know that Rodell is like a skunk. He can't do much damage, but he could sure stink up the place. "I'll tell you what. Why don't you tell Mr. Parjeter that if he's worried he should come on over here and see for himself?"

Rodell studies me for a minute. He's not equipped to argue in a rational way, and it's rarely called for. "Maybe I'll just do that," he says.

Then I have an idea how I can soothe Rodell's feathers and find out something at the same time. "Rodell, you being the law around here, maybe you can answer a question. Has anybody mentioned seeing somebody out here with a fancy car that they didn't recognize?"

Rodell ponders the question. "I don't recall such a thing. I'm going to have to ask my lieutenants about that. How come you want to know?"

"Dora Lee told me she saw somebody driving past her place more than once that kind of spooked her."

Rodell squints his eyes. "I fail to see how that's any of your affair. You leave it to me and my men to figure out what's been going on out here."

"Rodell, I'm going to do just that. I know you're working hard at it."

He stares at me for a minute, trying to work out if I'm being a smartass, but he can't make anything out of what I said. Finally he says, "You got that right. I'm on it." He slides back into the car and peels out.

Late in the afternoon the coroner's office calls to say I can send somebody to come and pick up Dora Lee's body. A sense of relief goes through me. I'm glad to get her out of the hands of people she didn't know. I call Ernest Landau and he says they'll send somebody up right away to take care of her. I appreciate the way he says, "take care of her." He knows the right lingo.

He asks me if I could bring the boy down to select a casket and go over a few things. I tell him I'll have him down there soon and ask him not to bring up the issue of money with the boy, just to leave that part to me.

I expect Greg to balk when I tell him we need to pick a casket and make some decisions down at the funeral home, but he says he guesses it has to be done. Without me telling him to he goes to his little shack and comes back wearing a clean pair of pants and a button shirt.

It turns out that the boy has opinions about the casket and the music and the way the service should go. He privately tells me he's not sure Dora Lee would have wanted Duckworth to perform the service. I tell him I agree with him, but that some things just have to be left the best they can be. It would cause a big commotion if we rattled that cage. He holds out a little longer, but seeing as how he doesn't know anybody better, he agrees.

Back at the house the refrigerator is full of casseroles and sweets, but suddenly I have an appetite for a good steak. "Look here, Greg. What would you think about going over to the steakhouse in Bobtail to get something to eat?"

He gets real still and I suspect he's worried about how to pay for his end of things.

"It's on me. I don't think I can face a tuna casserole."

He manages a grin. "I know what you mean."

"Let me ask you this. Have you got a girlfriend, or a friend you'd like to invite to come along?"

His face gets as red as a fire truck. "Nossir, I kind of stick to myself."

"Do you mind if I invite Jenny Sandstone? You may yet end up needing her law services, and it wouldn't hurt to get to know her."

He says that's fine with him. On the way to my place, we swing by Jenny's office. It's closed up tight, but since she lives right next door to me I can kill two birds with one rock. When I phone, she admits she was facing leftovers and is pleased to go with us.

While we wait for her to get ready, I take Greg with me down to the pasture to check on the cows. One of them has a little pebble stuck in its hoof and I take the time to whittle it out with my pocketknife.

Like all women I've known, Jenny takes a while to get ready, but finally she calls and we go and pick her up. It's a squeeze getting the three of us into the truck, but Jenny smells good and is in a fine humor, and nobody seems to mind being a little crowded. We have a pleasant evening. Jenny manages to put the boy at ease and none of us brings up the matter of Dora Lee's murder. For my part I enjoy the steak and feel livelier than I have in some time. I'm guessing it has something to do with suddenly being handed a purpose.

CHAPTER 7

Saturday morning, Loretta comes back out and has to get caught up on every detail of the funeral arrangements. I ask her if she would mind figuring out what clothes to put Dora Lee in for her final resting. She tells me she'll be proud to do it. "But you know Ida Ruth was Dora Lee's best friend and she got back last night from Waco. I better call her to come out here and help me, or she'll get her feelings hurt."

"I'm glad you thought of it. And that reminds me of something else. You remember Dora Lee had a daughter that moved out to California? Well, I'm having trouble locating her. You reckon Ida would know anything about that?"

"You can ask her when she gets here."

I get on back to Dora Lee's office. I didn't get through all the papers yesterday, and it's time to tackle that. It takes me twenty minutes to figure out what happened to Dora Lee's money. Apparently, the reason Teague took out a big mortgage on the house before he died was to cover his medical expenses. I'd known Teague had diabetes, but I didn't know how it ravaged his body and that he didn't have any health insurance. Although Dora Lee had some money left over after he died, and she was frugal, keeping up mortgage payments had slowly leeched away her funds.

By the time I hear Ida Ruth come in the back door, I'm feeling mighty low, thinking how worried Dora Lee must have been in her last year.

I greet Ida Ruth and ask her if I can talk to her after they've picked out the burial clothes for Dora Lee.

She and Loretta make a tour of the house, exclaiming over the quilts, wondering what's to be done with them. They finally disappear into Dora Lee's room, and I go back to my sad work. I make a list of Dora Lee's outstanding bills, among which is a loan she took out from her brother-in-law, Leslie. I can imagine the blow it must have been to her pride to have to go to him for help. That explains why he was interested in her will; he wants to be sure he gets paid back.

The women take their sweet time, and by the time they're done it's almost noon. Loretta heats up a tuna casserole and the three of us sit down to eat.

"Ida, how long did you and Dora Lee know each other?"

Ida Ruth is a large, unattractive woman with big teeth and a burn scar along her left ear where a kerosene stove exploded next to her when she was a girl. She has a habit of listening with her head cocked, as if she's got trouble with her hearing. "How long? Forty years we've known each other. Ever since Earl and I moved here and joined the Baptist Church. Dora Lee and I quilted together and raised our kids together." She stops to take off her glasses and wipe her eyes. "Lord, I'm going to miss her. How could that boy have done such a thing?"

"Ida Ruth, it's time to put a stop to this. I don't know who's been pumping up the rumor that her grandson killed her, but there's not a shred of evidence that he did any such thing."

"They say he wanted the money from the farm. That he's going to up and sell it and go off somewhere."

"I don't know who *they* are, but *they* don't know what they're talking about," I say.

She sniffs and exchanges a glance with Loretta, who looks nervous. Ida Ruth has a reputation for being scrappy if she's crossed. Loretta won't want to get into it with her, but there's nothing to stop me from wading in.

"It's up to you to stop rumors like this, so I'm going to tell you the truth. The truth is, Dora Lee didn't have a dime. The property is mortgaged and even if it's sold, there won't be much left over."

Loretta claps her hand over her mouth and Ida Ruth falls back in her seat as if I've struck her. Loretta has told me in the past that every old woman's worst fear is being left destitute.

"Didn't have a dime? She never let on," Ida Ruth says.

"We were all fooled," I say.

"Then the boy probably didn't know either," Ida says, tapping the table firmly. "Young boys don't know a thing about finances. He probably thought she was rich."

"He knew she had no money. Dora Lee wanted to send him off to art school, but he said she couldn't afford it."

"Big ideas," Ida Ruth says. "What did he need to go to art school for anyway? He had lessons from one of his teachers. And Dora Lee told me she paid a pretty penny for it."

"I'm not arguing that he should go to art school. I'm just saying Greg knew she didn't have money, so there's no motive to kill her."

"Then who did kill her?"

"We'll have to see about that," I say. "Did Dora Lee tell you she was scared somebody was spying on her?"

"Spying on her? Who would do such of a thing?"

"She didn't tell you she'd seen somebody driving by that didn't belong out here?"

Her mouth is full of tuna casserole, so she nods her head until she swallows. "Oh, you mean that kind of spying. She did mention that to me. You think it was somebody biding their time before they killed her?"

"It seems strange, that's all," I say. "One more thing. You know anything about a trip she took to Houston a couple of weeks ago?"

"Houston? Yes, I believe she said she had to go get a few things."

"What kind of things?"

"Samuel, I'm not Mrs. Nosy. I didn't ask her. We all have to run over there time to time, isn't that right, Loretta?"

"You can't buy a thing around here. Even in Bobtail, there's only a couple of dress stores and their prices are sky high, unless you want to go to the Walmart."

"Can you imagine Dora Lee dressing herself from the Walmart?" The women exchange raised eyebrows. "She may not have had much, but she knew how to find good clothes on sale."

"Did Dora Lee say anything about her daughter Caroline moving to Houston?"

Ida Ruth's mouth drops open and little spots of red come up in her cheeks. "Caroline was moving to Houston? Dora Lee never said a word about it. Why would she keep something like that from me?"

Loretta heaps another helping of casserole onto Ida's plate. "Now Ida Ruth, I didn't know Dora Lee the way you did, but wouldn't you think that if Caroline moved back Dora Lee might want to see how it worked out between them before she started in talking about it?"

"That's probably exactly right," Ida Ruth says. "How'd you know Caroline was coming back?" she says to me.

I tell her about the letter I found. "Caroline should be contacted and told what happened. But I can't find how to reach her. Do you know if Caroline has kept up with anybody in town? Maybe somebody she went to school with?"

Ida Ruth takes a bite and chews slowly while she thinks. "Well, there's Maddie Hicks. You remember her; she was the Dobbs's girl. Since her husband cleared out, she makes a living doing people's hair in her house. She's pretty good at it, too. Even if Maddie hasn't kept up with Caroline, she might know who has. Let me get you that phone number." She pulls out a little address book that is the twin of Dora Lee's and gives me the number.

Before Ida Ruth leaves, she and Loretta insist that I pass judgment on the clothes they've picked out for Dora Lee to wear. I go out and get Greg to put in his two cents' worth, and it turns out I'm glad I did. When he sees the handsome blue outfit they've arranged on the bed, he reaches his hand out and touches it, gently, for just the barest moment. But it's enough. A boy who has killed his grandmother is not going to want to touch the clothes she's being laid to rest in. Ida Ruth has to turn away and blow her nose.

I call Maddie Hicks and she says she can see me at one thirty, but that she has a lady coming at two o'clock for a permanent, so not to be late. I set Greg to watering Dora Lee's garden and take off.

Maddie's house is a doublewide set up on blocks. She's losing a war with weeds in the yard. Out front a hand-painted sign says, *Maddie's Beauty Shop*. No fancy name, and my guess is the beauty school she went to is called Learn-As-You-Go.

When she finally comes to the door, Maddie is carrying a cigarette and a lighter. "Let's sit outside in the back," she says. "I can't even smoke in my own house. My daughter lives here with me with her two kids, and she won't have me smoking. I don't know where she gets those ideas." She's a heavy-stacked woman with a bad complexion and her hair done in a fluffy style better suited for somebody twenty years younger.

We go around back where the weeds have been beaten down in spots. Next to a rusted-out barbecue cooker a couple of lawn chairs are set up under a big old pecan tree. We sit down and Maddie lights up. It doesn't take me more than a couple minutes to find out that she likes to talk. That suits me fine—if she knows anything I need to hear.

She rattles on about how afraid everybody in town is that whoever killed Dora Lee is coming to get them next. She says she and her daughter are thinking about putting in a deadbolt lock.

As soon as I can get a word in, I ask if she has kept up with Caroline Parjeter.

"Caroline was a wild thing when she was a girl. Me and her had some good old times. We used to go out to the roadhouse—remember that place out near Cotton Hill?—and we'd dance our butts off. That's where I met my husband, which doesn't speak highly for it. I guess that old place is fallen down now, though I heard somebody is thinking about restoring it. I don't know who they think would come, though. Kids these days want to go to San Antonio or Austin. They tear up the road between here and there. I don't see how they can have any better times than we used to have right here."

"When was the last time you heard from Caroline?"

"Let me think," she says. "You know how it is, you think it's only been a couple months since you talked to somebody and come to find out it's been five years."

She talks on like that and I wonder how she can think and talk at the same time, but all of a sudden she says, "I guess it was a couple of years ago now, when she got married."

"She never!" I say.

"Yes, she did. Married some old boy from Beaumont."

"Did her mamma know?"

Maddie sighs. "Mr. Craddock," she says, "I didn't like the way she treated her mamma, and I told her so more than once. But she told me she had her reasons, and I figured she had her own life to live and it wasn't much of my business."

"So she didn't tell Dora Lee she got married."

Maddie squints from smoke as she exhales. "I don't know the answer to that. But I'll tell you the honest truth, I thought there was something funny about her getting married so late. It wasn't like she wanted kids or anything. I asked her why was she getting married and she said she'd found a man who could take care of her."

"And that's the last you heard?"

"It is."

"Did she write you or call you?"

"She sent me an announcement. I thought about calling her, but I didn't know what I'd say to her. You know some people you can talk to after ten years and it's like you just saw them last week and you have plenty to say. It wasn't like that with Caroline. We just have different lives, I guess."

"Would you happen to have the announcement? I need to get in touch with her and let her know her mamma died."

"I'll see if I can find it." She looks at her watch. "I don't know if I can lay hands on it before my two o'clock comes, but I'll go see."

While she's gone, I think about how maybe not having kids wasn't the worst thing that could have happened to Jeanne and me. If we'd had a daughter who left us like Caroline did, it would have been terrible. I wouldn't have wanted to see Jeanne sad like Dora Lee was.

Maddie hollers from around front of the trailer. I get up, unkink my knee and walk to the front steps.

She's holding an envelope out to me. "This is your lucky day," she says. "It's not often I can put my hands on anything I'm looking for."

"Just in time, too," I say. A car has stopped in front and a lady I have a nodding acquaintance with is easing herself out. I go over and hold the door and we exchange a few words.

"I'll get this back to you," I say, waving the envelope at Maddie.

In my truck I take a look at the announcement. It's on standard white stock, nothing fancy, saying she's married a man named Martin Wells.

I stop by my place to use my phone to try to find Caroline under her new name. It's not easy, because there are lots of Wells in the Houston area. I'm grateful she didn't marry a Smith. Most of the people I talk to answer right off that they don't know any Dora Lee Parjeter. But after a while, I reach a woman named Caroline Wells who pauses when I ask if she's related to Dora Lee. Finally she says, "Yes."

Not, yes she's my mamma, or yes, is something wrong . . . just "yes."

I tell her who I am. "I've had the devil of a time trying to find you. I thought you should know your Mamma was found dead Thursday."

"Oh? Was it her heart?" She doesn't sound particularly moved by the news that her mother is dead. She has a different kind of accent, like someone who has been gone from Texas a long time.

"No, ma'am. I'm sorry to tell you she was murdered."

"Murdered! Who would do something like that? Do they know who did it?" Although she sounds shocked, we could be talking about something that happened to a stranger.

"Not yet."

There's a long pause. "I'm sorry, who did you say I'm speaking to?"

I tell her again. "I was a friend of your mamma's."

Her voice warms up. "I remember you. I remember your wife, Jeanne. She's one of the nicest people I ever met. How is she?"

"She's no longer with us. She passed away last year from cancer."

"Oh, that's terrible. She was good to me when I needed a friend." If Caroline had wanted to get on my good side she couldn't have picked a better way than through Jeanne.

She asks when and where Dora Lee's funeral will be. I tell her, and suggest that it might be nice if she comes Sunday night for visitation.

"Is there a motel around there?"

"We have a new Holiday Inn Express on the east side on the way to Bryan. But you could stay out at Dora Lee's house." And then I realize that I have no idea if Caroline even knows her sister is dead and that Greg lives out there. "You know your nephew lives out there?"

"Mother told me," she says. So Caroline did have some contact with Dora Lee, although I know she didn't come back home for her sister's funeral.

I ask her if she wants me to make her a reservation at the hotel, but she says she'll tend to it.

I'm itching to know if Dora Lee went to Houston to see Caroline, so I slip in the question. "How long has it been since you've seen your mamma?"

There's a long silence. "Not since I left home."

"She didn't come to Houston to see you?"

"I had been planning on getting together with her, but I hadn't been able to arrange it." With her tone of voice, I don't need any air-conditioning to cool things down.

"Well, you let me know if you can be here Sunday, and I'll see to it there's a meal on the table."

"I'll have to think about it," she says.

Her coming to sit at the funeral home with her mamma's body is the least she can do, but she has already done the least she can do, which is abandon her mamma. Even I didn't do that, and I had every reason in the world to. Mamma treated my daddy and us two boys like we were snakes who had slithered into her house when she wasn't looking. It took me until I was grown before I put together my daddy's drinking with my mamma's meanness. And even longer before I realized she must have had something mentally wrong with her to act the way she did. Still, when she was dying, I stayed by her every minute I could, with Jeanne right next to me.

For the millionth time I wonder, how did I get so lucky to meet and marry Jeanne? And for her not to mind that I wanted to bring her to live in this small town. I went to college at Texas A&M. I chose it because it was the closest college to Jarrett Creek, and I could come home weekends and help my daddy with the cattle. Then in my last year I met Jeanne. We were married for forty years. I don't believe a couple was ever more suited to one another.

Thinking of Jeanne puts me in mind of another call I could make. I've been mulling over why Clyde Underwood would take a notion to buy Dora Lee's property. In these parts, if a property suddenly seems to be valuable, the first thing you think of is oil and gas. My brother-in-law, DeWitt Simms, is retired, but he still has a lot of connections. The truth is, I have connections, too, but I'd like to talk to DeWitt. He's living out in the hill country in a place called Horseshoe Bay. His answering machine says he's out "probably on the golf course," so I leave a message for him to call me, giving him Dora Lee's phone number as well as my own.

Before I leave for Dora Lee's I go back down to the pasture to check up on the cows. They gather around me like I'm an old friend, which I guess I have been since Jeanne died. I walk by the tank and decide I'm still not ready to give up and let Jenny run her horses here.

As I get into my truck I admit to myself that after only a couple of nights at Dora Lee's I'm ready to come back home. But I'll stay out at the farm a little longer, until I can sit down with Greg and figure out what's to be done with Dora Lee's place and how he's going to make his way. But then I realize maybe it's Caroline I'll have to deal with. Dora Lee's place will be her property now as well as Greg's. From the way she dealt with her mamma, I have a feeling she won't be on friendly terms with her nephew.

But the biggest reason for me to stay out there is to continue to dig around in what Dora Lee has left behind, to find any clues as to who killed her.

CHAPTER 8

When I get out to Dora Lee's, there's a hulking, black Acura SUV pulled up next to the house with a license plate number that's not from around here. The license plate holder has a Houston dealer's name. For a minute, I wonder if Caroline has decided to come right away. But then I realize there's no way she could have made it here so fast.

I go around back to the kitchen door. It's late afternoon and the sun hasn't let up, and as I walk into the kitchen I take off my hat and mop my brow. I surprise a man who is standing with the refrigerator door open. Closing in on fifty, with extra girth and an extra chin, he's dressed for town in a shirt and tie and wing tip shoes. He's got a good head of hair with some gray in it, and thick eyebrows.

"Sorry to barge in on you, I'm Samuel Craddock." I put out my hand and he takes it up with a nice firm grip.

"No, I'm the one to apologize for making myself at home. I'm Wayne Jackson, Dora Lee's nephew."

"Would you be Leslie's boy?" I wonder why he has a different name from Leslie's.

"That's right. Daddy called to tell me what happened to Dora Lee. I live in Houston, not that far away, and he asked me to come and see what needed to be done to take care of things, maybe help out Dora Lee's grandson. He said you shouldn't have to be putting yourself out."

I tell him it was no trouble, and realize he's saying in a polite way that I should clear out. I think of that stack of Dora Lee's papers and wish I had taken a closer look at them this morning when I wasn't so tired, in case I missed something. But I really have no rights here. It's fitting that someone from the family should take care of Dora

Lee's business. I feel like the Wizard of Oz with the curtain pulled back.

"I was just going to get myself a cold drink," he says. "You want anything?"

I show him the iced tea Loretta left and he fills a couple of glasses.

"Did you meet Dora Lee's grandson, Greg?" I say.

"I did. He was in here getting himself some lunch when I came in. Seems like a good kid. Reminds me of my oldest boy."

"Dora Lee thought the world of him. Come on back and let me show you what I've been up to," I say. "Might save you some time."

We leave our tea on the counter and go back to the room where I've gotten everything organized. I show him the stacks I've made of her papers, and give him the list of people I've called. "The only close family Dora Lee has left is her sister in Virginia and she can't make it out for the funeral," I say.

"That's like my sister Lou," he says. "She and her husband are back in North Carolina, and they're not going to make the trip."

"How come you have a different name from your daddy?" I say.

He puts his hands in his pockets and jingles some coins. "My real daddy died when I was a few months old. Some kind of farm accident. I didn't know him at all, of course. My mamma married Leslie when I was two and he raised me like I was his own."

I wonder why Leslie didn't give the boy his last name, but you can only take curiosity so far. "Your mamma still living?" I ask.

He gives me a tight smile. "Yes. She's over in Sugarland."

I can see I've stepped into shaky territory, so I move on and tell Wayne I haven't been able to find a will in Dora Lee's papers. "If she didn't have a will, I expect what she has goes to her daughter, Caroline, and the boy."

"Caroline," he says and gives a bark of laughter. "She was a wild little thing. I only saw her a few times when we were kids. My daddy and her daddy didn't get along well. Didn't she move out to California and nobody ever heard anything from her?"

"Yes, she was in California for a long time. I had the devil of time locating her to tell her about Dora Lee. Turns out she's living in Houston now."

"Is that right? I'll have to look her up." He's jingling those coins again.

"I talked to her this afternoon, just before I came out here. I have her telephone number if you want to call her." I pull out my notes and write down the number for him. I also write down my name and number.

"Is she coming to the funeral?"

"She didn't say one way or another. She hasn't seen her mamma in a long time."

"Seems like she'd want to come out here. She'll inherit the farm and if it was me, I'd want to look things over." His face is starting to get red, like he's flustered. I think about what Dora Lee told me about Leslie Parjeter being so stingy, and I wonder if Leslie has sent his son here to see if he can scrounge a little something out of the estate for himself.

"Caroline didn't seem all that interested. Anyway, the inheritance isn't going to amount to much. Dora Lee owed a lot on the farm."

"That's too bad. I guess I should find out what Caroline's plans are." He gestures toward the papers on the desk. "I wouldn't want her to think I'm overstepping myself being here."

"I expect she'll be glad of the help," I say. "There's one thing I ought to show you." I find the letter from Clyde Underwood and hand it to him. "I know a little bit about land around here, and this is a low-ball offer. Whoever arranges to sell it can do better than that."

He looks over the letter, his bushy eyebrows almost meeting in the middle with the frown on his face. "I do appreciate your letting me know," he says. "I'll bear this in mind."

He's got a friendly way about him, but I get the feeling he's ready for me to be gone. But he needs to know one more thing. So I tell him about Greg being taken for questioning and me getting him out of jail.

Jackson frowns. "You don't think there's anything to it? About the boy, I mean?"

"No, I do not. I think you'll find he's a fine boy who loved his grandmother. Don't let Rodell get away with anything. That's Rodell Skinner, he's the chief of police and a man inclined to take the easy way out. He may think prosecuting your cousin Greg is going to tidy up the business of who killed Dora Lee without him having to work too hard. Which means the real killer would get away."

He nods, but I'm not sure he gets it. With a jingle of coins, he starts easing toward the hallway.

"If you have any questions, you let me know," I tell him, "Now I'll just pack my things and get out of your way."

"Take your time," he says. "I'll be in the kitchen."

I go into Dora Lee's bedroom to put my things back in my duffle, and I notice that Jackson has already set his big suitcase in here, up against one wall. My mind is working overtime, knowing this may be my last chance to get a close-up look at Dora Lee's things. I open the closet door. The idea of Caroline's wedding announcement has been eating at me. When I was going through Dora Lee's papers, I didn't find any little sentimental mementos, like birthday cards or shower invitations or letters from old friends. I'm thinking Dora Lee might have kept her sentimental belongings separate from her business papers. A few months after Jeanne died I was just about knocked over when I found a couple of shoeboxes in the closet filled with every letter and every valentine anybody ever sent her.

Dora Lee has several shoeboxes on the closet shelf above her clothes. My intended theft makes me so nervous that I fumble with the lids of the shoeboxes, scared Jackson is going to barge in to find out what's taking me so long and find me rummaging around. After looking through the first few boxes and finding only shoes, I step into the bathroom and flush the toilet. If he thinks I was in the can that should give me a little more time.

Sure enough, at one end of the shelf I find a couple of boxes full of cards. The boxes won't fit in my bag, so I spill the contents into my duffle and put the empty boxes back on the shelf.

When I get to the kitchen, I tell Jackson I'm just going to stop and say goodbye to Greg. "I'll see you at the visitation tomorrow night," I say. "And if there's anything I can do to grease any wheels for you, just let me know."

I throw the duffle into my truck, relieved that the evidence of my theft is out of sight. Then I go see Greg, whose eyes are all lit up.

"You're looking pleased with yourself," I say. "You glad to have your cousin Wayne to take over here?" I don't like the little jealous feeling that's snuck up on me.

"Wayne says he's going to help me find work. I'm thinking I might get a job in an art store in Houston. And maybe I can put by enough money to get some classes."

"That would be fine, all right," I say. But I suspect that Jackson and his daddy have cooked up plans to stick Greg out at Leslie Parjeter's farm.

On my way home, I worry about how I'm going to figure out who killed Dora Lee now that I don't have access to her affairs.

As I walk in the front door, the phone is ringing and it's my brother-in-law, DeWitt, returning my call.

"When are you going to come over to God's country and let me teach you how to play golf?" he says.

I've always liked Jeanne's brother, and I'm tickled that he has made such a fine retirement for himself. "You won't get me to use those snake-killing sticks," I say, "But I'd like to walk around the course with you."

He laughs his big, hearty laugh and asks how I'm getting on. I tell him I'm doing fine and then I get down to business. I tell him about Dora Lee's death, and about finding Clyde Underwood's letter offering to buy the farm. "There's something funny about that," I say. "The man's already got a big spread that's just sitting there. So what would he want with another chunk of land that as far as I can tell doesn't recommend itself?"

"Have you walked the land?" He means have I gone over the property to see if there's any evidence that there might be oil or gas under the ground.

"No, I haven't, but I've never seen or heard of any land around there being good for much."

"Could be it's got natural gas. You know, back when we were in the business, getting gas out of the land was more trouble and expense than it was worth. But with oil prices what they are, that's changed. And I know they found a fair-sized gas field not that far west of Jarrett County a few years ago."

"Yeah, I heard about that, but I haven't heard that it extends this far."

"You want me to drive over there and walk the land with you?"

He sounds hopeful, so I tell him that's exactly what I was hoping he'd say.

"What about tomorrow?" he says.

"You don't play golf on Sunday?"

"Hell, no! Never on Sunday. Around here, with the weekend people coming from Austin, it's too crowded on the course." So we agree he'll come tomorrow.

I ask him to bring his wife, Lucille, but he says she's not going anywhere these days. I tell him I'm sorry to hear that, and to tell her hello for me. There's nothing wrong with Lucille physically, but she has spells when she gets anxious and can't leave the house. DeWitt has made his accommodation with that through the years.

I've been kicking around that business with the art teacher, Mr. Eubanks, wondering how I can find out a little more about him. Not having any kids of my own, I never knew the workings of the school system in Jarrett County, so I don't know who to call to find out any more about it. But it strikes me that Jenny Sandstone is from Bobtail, and maybe she can dig up something. It's a Saturday night, so she might be out, but I give her a try.

She does answer her phone, and I tell her what I want to know.

"That's a matter for my mother," Jenny says. "She taught high school social studies in Bobtail for thirty years. She's retired now, but if she doesn't know anything about this Eubanks fellow, she'll know who to call to find out."

While I wait for her to call back, I get busy. This is the first chance I've had to go through the paraphernalia I took from the shoeboxes at Dora Lee's. I get the duffle out and spill everything onto the dining room table.

By the time I'm done, I'm good and depressed. There's nothing like going through a woman's sentimental holdings to give you the blues. Dora Lee's life has been whittled down to a thin line, from being a little girl, to courting and being married, to having kids, then the one grand-child, and then beginning that final slide to becoming obsolete.

As is my way, I've sorted things into stacks. In a pile to itself are the wedding announcements for her daughter Julie and the one for Caroline. The one for Julie is accompanied by newspaper clippings about the wedding, shower announcements, and the like. The one for Caroline stands alone. But I'm glad Caroline at least sent her one.

There are bright spots in the mementos that have nothing to do with her family. I had forgotten that the quilt Dora Lee kept on her bed won a prize. She was puffed up about that for a month.

There are clippings about the accident that killed Dora Lee's daughter Julie and her husband, and one about Greg's graduation from high school in Bobtail. It would have been easier on Dora Lee if Greg had transferred to Jarrett Creek High School. Then the school bus would have picked him up. But Dora Lee wanted him to continue to go to the same school he was in when his folks died. The Bobtail school bus wouldn't go out to Cotton Hill to pick him up, so she drove him back and forth to Bobtail every single day for two years.

The valentines and birthday cards are in a stack to themselves, homemade cards made by the girls when they were little, going up until the cards are store bought and have awkward teenage sentiments scribbled above their names. I wonder if Caroline will want to see them and wonder if they mean anything to her. I notice there are no cards from Teague and that makes me think about how I used to make such a fuss for Jeanne over Valentine's Day and her birthday. I guess Teague was as stingy with affection as his brother Leslie is with money. Or maybe Dora Lee couldn't stand to keep things from Teague. The way he treated her would have outweighed any sentimental card he might have given her.

Another stack is for pictures, mostly school pictures of the girls, but also some of Dora Lee and Teague when they were young. I'd forgotten that Teague was quite the ladies' man. He was good-looking in an oily kind of way.

Most of the Christmas cards are from family. But a few, yellowed with age, are from people I never heard of, and sound like they were written by youngsters. For a couple of years when Dora Lee was a teenager, her daddy took his family off to Austin to live while he worked on a construction job there. As soon as the job ended, they high-tailed it back here. But for a few years Dora Lee must have kept up with girls she met in school in Austin.

There's one clipping that I don't know what to make of. It's an obituary of an artist named William Kern who I never heard of; he died a few years ago. He lived around Fredericksburg. I wonder if Dora Lee knew him. I conjure up an old romance from when she lived in Austin that made her doubly happy when she found out her grandson was inclined to art.

Dora Lee kept all the school pictures of the girls. Caroline had a way of looking at the camera as if challenging the photographer to see her sexy side. By contrast, Julie was a wholesome girl, not as pretty, but with a cheerful smile. I put rubber bands around the stacks and stuff them back into the duffle. I'll give it to Caroline to dispense with as she pleases.

It's an hour later, and getting on for dusk, when Jenny gets back to me. "Sorry it took so long. Mother tends to be long-winded. I expect that's why I'm not partial to small talk."

"She able to tell you anything?"

"Alex Eubanks is a peacock. Apparently he's won a couple of awards in some art shows, and if he offers to give somebody lessons, he thinks he's doing them a big favor. He got riled up when Dora Lee wouldn't pay for lessons anymore." In other words, no new information, but at least it confirms what I know about him.

After I hang up, I walk around the house feeling restless. I'm stirred up with the idea of investigating Dora Lee's murder, but I feel off my game, not sure I can trust my instincts. It won't be any good if I chase off after everybody who looked cross-eyed at Dora Lee. But I also need to be careful to not dismiss a suspect too easily. I'm going to have to look into this Eubanks fellow.

CHAPTER 9

When I phone Wayne Jackson early next morning he says it's fine with him if DeWitt and I walk the property. In fact, he says he's grateful to me, in case there's more to the land than meets the eye.

DeWitt arrives around nine o'clock and I'm glad to see him. He reminds me of Jeanne. She was a thin little whip of a woman and DeWitt has that same body type, although he's a good deal taller. He has her same bright bird eyes that seem to dart around and see everything. And when they light on you, they're full of mischief and warmth. "Well, you haven't let everything go to hell too much," he says, surveying my living room.

"Jeanne trained me well."

He laughs. "Those pictures make me think of Jeanne. I never saw anybody who loved art the way she and our mamma did. Never took with me, but she and mamma wore a path to the museum."

We drink a cup of coffee. I answer a phone call from Loretta, who saw DeWitt's Lincoln parked in front of my place and has to know who's visiting me. I tell her what it is we're up to and tease her by asking if she wants to go out and walk with us for a couple of hours. She acts all ruffled, and asks me how I can even think such a thing, but then she catches on and laughs.

On the way out to Dora Lee's, I fill DeWitt in on the situation.

"I made a couple phone calls yesterday," DeWitt says. "Nobody knows of any project going on out here, but they'll check it out and get back to me."

Even his voice reminds me of Jeanne, and I smile to myself as he talks.

As soon as we pull in, I see that the garden is drooping. You have to water every morning in this heat. When I check in with Jackson, I mention the garden. He says he doesn't know anything about gardens, but I don't know how that can be true since he was raised on a farm. From what little I know about Leslie Parjeter, I suspect he worked his stepson to within an inch of his life, and when Jackson managed to get off the farm, he vowed to never have another thing to do with farm work.

Jackson disappears inside, and DeWitt and I get started off to examine the land. It's hot as blazes, but in our time we've done this in all kinds of weather. We're both as eager to be back on the job as if we were still in our prime. Our job is made a good bit easier because her land has no trees to speak of. If you're trying to assess land through stands of post oak, you've got your work cut out. But this is pasture-land, spreading out in undulating hillocks.

What we do when we walk the land is look for traces of shale and smell for gas. Pure natural gas doesn't have an odor, but often gas deposits have sour portions that smell of rotten eggs. And you sometimes don't see the shale, but it usually noses out at the surface somewhere on a property. Between looking and smelling, you can generally spot the signs. But even if we don't see or smell signs of gas, we'll take some soil samples here and there and have them tested.

DeWitt and I spread out to within hollering distance of each other and walk parallel. The property is about twenty acres and takes us the best part of two hours. Down at the back there is a boggy area, which surprises me. It has a scraggly stand of trees around it, and if you were selling mosquitoes by the pound, you'd have a bumper crop. By the time we start back, both drenched in sweat and thirsty, we have to admit we've seen and smelled nothing that would warrant further investigation. DeWitt says he'll run the soil samples over to Austin tomorrow, but neither of us thinks anything will come of it.

When we get back to the house, a rusted out old hulk of a Ford Fairlane is sitting in the driveway. It would be a classic if it was fixed up. A pinch-faced old man is just climbing out of it. DeWitt and I walk over to greet him.

"I bet you're Leslie Parjeter," I say.

The old man admits that he is. He reaches into the back seat and takes out a faded cardboard suitcase that has to be as old as he is.

"Help you carry something?" I say.

He looks me up and down with suspicion. "I'll hang onto my case," he says.

Inside, Jackson spares us a drink of water, but doesn't offer anything more in spite of the fact that he's eager to know what we found out. I think about all those casseroles lined up in the refrigerator. Not that I want any of them, but it rankles me that he doesn't offer.

I tell Jackson we didn't see anything on our survey of the land that would make us jump up and holler.

"Well, I thank you for taking the time," he says. We're standing in the kitchen. He hasn't offered us a seat.

Leslie Parjeter has been listening with great interest to our exchange. "You all was looking for oil on Dora Lee's land?"

"Natural gas, more likely," DeWitt says. "But we didn't find any sign of it."

"Be a fine thing if Dora Lee was sitting on property that was worth something," Parjeter says.

"Daddy, I don't know why you care anything about that. You don't have any stake in it."

"You don't know that for a fact. Has anybody found a will?"

Jackson and I both say no at the same time. I'm hit by a gut reaction to the idea of Jackson pawing through Dora Lee's papers. "I wouldn't worry," I say to Parjeter, "You'll have your loan paid back."

"So you know all about that, do you?" he says, his shrewd eyes taking me in.

"I know Dora Lee would want her debts paid," I say.

Parjeter's eyes swivel to his son. "Unlike some."

Jackson's jaw clenches, and I feel like all the air has been sucked out of the room.

I don't like being witness to a grown man being treated like a truant schoolboy, so I ask Jackson if he got around to calling his cousin Caroline.

Jackson's smile looks like he's been sucking a lemon. "I've had some business to tend to, and haven't had time."

"You *better* tend to business," Parjeter says.

DeWitt and I make a quick exit after that, and head over to the Ranchero, a pretty good Mexican café in town. We talk old times, and he tells me a couple of stories I've never heard, or have forgotten, about Jeanne when she was a youngster. It seems like five o'clock rolls around too fast. DeWitt wants to get home before dark.

"Lucille gets nervous when the light goes," he says.

CHAPTER 10

Ernest Landau has put out a flier around town saying that visitation at the funeral home for Dora Lee is from six to nine tonight. I get there about seven and see that a good many people have already stopped by and signed the book. I'm not surprised that Ida Ruth has set herself up to greet visitors. But I am surprised to see that Greg is with her in the front room. Ida Ruth has her arm through his, that way signaling to all who want to know that she is convinced that this boy had nothing to do with his grandma's death. I hope I haven't set both of us up for a fall.

Loretta is settled in talking to some church ladies, and I stop and say a few words to them. Then I proceed into the chapel to take a look at how they've fixed up Dora Lee. I'm glad to see a good number of flower arrangements. Dora Lee would have liked that. The spray that I asked Ernest to order for me with yellow flowers is here. Justine down at the flower shop has a good instinct for her work.

Dora Lee looks good, although her mouth is set in a way that makes her look peeved. And maybe that's as it should be, the way she died. Viewing of people's dead bodies is probably an odd custom, but the once or twice I've known people who insisted on being cremated, I felt an itchy sense that something was left undone. It's not a religious thing with me. Jeanne would have liked me to be a believer, but I told her that leap of faith was just too wide for me. I'd go to church with her when she wanted me to, and that's the way we worked it out.

As I'm standing quietly, thinking my thoughts about Dora Lee and her life, I hear a little ruffle of sound in the front room that alerts me. It's like a rush of swallows in an evening out near the tank. I turn around and look toward the door. A woman is standing poised there, and for a second I catch my breath. It could be Dora Lee twenty years ago, but in a different kind of life. The woman, Caroline, I'm sure of it, is dressed in a black suit and high heels and has a polished look that you see on TV women. I don't know fashion, but the suit has a cut that takes advantage of every curve of Caroline's body without being showy. Her light brown hair falls soft and free just short of her shoulders. She's wearing pearls and carrying a compact little bag. She's way over-dressed for a visitation, and the other ladies won't forgive her for it.

I have a pang for Dora Lee, knowing how much she would have liked to see Caroline dressed to the nines. Dora Lee always liked to be well turned out. I wonder if Caroline knows that.

She walks slowly toward the casket and I step back to give her a chance to take a look at the mamma she hasn't seen in so many years. She stands for a long time; long enough for me to wonder what thoughts must be going through her head. There's no outward sign that she has the slightest reaction to Dora Lee. But then she steps back and I can see she's unsteady on her feet. I walk over and take her arm and help her to a seat on the front row of pews.

Up close, Caroline is a little frayed around the edges. She has circles under her eyes and her complexion is pale under her carefully done makeup. I sit down on the pew near her and settle back. After a while she looks over at me. "You must be Mr. Craddock." Her voice is like honey, which I didn't notice when we talked on the phone.

"Samuel," I say.

She glances toward the coffin, then back at me. "Samuel, then."

I move a little closer. "They did a good job with your mamma. She looks good."

She nods, but by the look in her eye, she's thinking about something else.

"Your nephew, Greg, picked out the box. I hope it suits you."

"It's fine," she says. Wafting with the words is the smell of liquor.

Sometimes I wonder why so many people, even from a small place like Jarrett Creek, feel the need to take the edge off their lives with drink. Boredom, disappointment, fear? There are mean drunks, like Caroline's daddy was, and weepy drunks, people who get silly, or those who turn into themselves. I figure she's the last kind. Or maybe she's not a drunk at all; maybe she just had to fortify herself for this ordeal.

"Did you get a place at the motel?" I ask.

She shakes her head. Her hair falls forward and she pushes it back.

"Then when you're done here, why don't you come out to my place? I've got plenty of room, and I won't bother you."

I see the hesitation in her eyes, but after a second she gives a quick nod.

I get up. "That's all right then. I'll leave you to yourself. I'll be in the parlor with the others. You take your time."

Now that evening church services are out, more people have arrived, standing around in little clumps. Ida Ruth hustles over to me as soon as she sees me. "I told everybody that Caroline is in with her mamma and to give her a little time to herself."

"That was real thoughtful of you. I think it's all right if they go on in."

Ida Ruth whispers to various people. I think about the fact that someone must have done this for me when I was in sitting with Jeanne, and I have to walk out on the porch to take a couple of deep breaths. I hear Reverend Duckworth at the other end of the porch, laughing. I look up to see him standing with two other men, all three smoking and looking relaxed. My aversion to Duckworth rises up in me and for two cents I'd go over there and punch him.

But none of the hard things are his fault, and I'm ashamed for taking out my grief on him, even in my thoughts.

When I duck back inside, Caroline has come back into the reception room and has been pounced on by Ida Ruth and two other church ladies. She glances at me with a look so full of despair that I have to look away. If Caroline's old friend Maddie Hicks were here, she might be able to take some of the slack, but I saw Maddie's name on the visitation sheet when I got here, so she's come and gone.

I look around and see that old Mrs. Ruggie has cornered Greg. She must be about ninety-five, and still as spry as a bird in her body, but her mind has long since left her behind. Her head is cocked to one side, looking for all the world like a little chickadee. Greg is nodding as if she were making sense.

I walk over to Caroline. "Can I steal her from you all?" I say to the ladies gathered around her. "I know she wanted to talk to her nephew a little bit."

The three ladies frown at me. They were just getting started on the questions.

I thank the ladies and steer Caroline over to Greg, and hear Mrs. Ruggie saying, "I got me a new hat." Greg is still nodding, but looks up as we approach and when he sees Caroline, his mouth falls open.

"Excuse me, Mrs. Ruggie. I just want to introduce these two. Caroline, this is your nephew, Greg Marcus."

Caroline offers her hand and Greg takes it, still staring at her. "It's nice to finally meet you," Caroline says.

Suddenly Ida Ruth is at my side. "Mrs. Ruggie, come on over here. I have to ask you something."

Dora Lee once told me Ida Ruth was a quality person, and I'm seeing her in action. Mrs. Ruggie toddles off with Ida Ruth, filling her in on her new hat.

Caroline and Greg can't seem to think of anything to say to one another right off, so I say, "Greg, I don't see Jackson. Did you come by yourself?"

He tears his eyes away from Caroline. Not only must Caroline remind him of his grandma, but there's probably something of his mamma there, too. "Wayne said it was all right if I drove Grandma's car. He said he had a lot to do and couldn't make it tonight, but he'll be at the funeral tomorrow."

"Are you talking about Wayne Jackson?" Caroline asks.

"Yes, your uncle Leslie's boy. He says he remembers you."

"Yes, I imagine he does." Her eyes have turned hard with whatever she's picking out from her memories. "Do you like him?" she says to Greg, startling both of us.

Greg blinks a couple of times. I can see he wants to make the right reply. "He's been friendly to me."

"Mmm," Caroline says.

"Caroline," I say, "Greg is a fine artist. I hope you get a chance to see some of his work while you're here."

"I hope so, too." She turns to me. "You didn't mention that Wayne Jackson was here when you called. What's his business in this?"

I tell her that I was as surprised as she was, that I only met Jackson yesterday, after I talked to her on the phone. "I went out to Dora Lee's and he had set up shop there. He says his daddy sent him."

She raises an eyebrow. "That sounds like him and his daddy."

I wait for her to say more, but her interest has gone back to Greg. She puts her hand up to his cheek. "You don't look much like your mother, but you remind me of her somehow."

Greg's face turns red and he starts to chew on his bottom lip.

I realize that people are wanting to leave, and are standing by to say "sorry" to Dora Lee's kin, so I step away. Caroline and Greg get their hands shaken and curious looks cast over them. Most of these people have known Dora Lee her whole life, and yet these two people who are closest kin to her are strangers to them.

Finally it's just a handful of people left. I tell Greg that Caroline is staying at my place. "You two have some things to talk about. You're welcome to get together in my kitchen, if you want."

Caroline says, "I'm dead tired. I think I'd like to wait until tomorrow, if that's okay." Her eyes are soft with her appeal, almost as if she's flirting with him.

"Sure is, ma'am," he says.

A little smile flits across her face. "You don't have to call me ma'am. Just Caroline."

"Be careful driving home by yourself," I say to Greg. "On Sunday nights people burn up the road to get back home after the weekend."

"You don't need to worry about me," he says. He's taken with his Aunt Caroline and wants to show he's a man.

"Hold on just a second," I say to Caroline as we start to leave. I go and tell Loretta I'm taking Caroline to my place for the night. "You suppose you could make some kind of coffee cake or something to bring over in the morning?"

"I guess I can do that." Her posture gets a little straighter.

Caroline follows me back to my place in her car, a Toyota that's seen better days. Its engine makes an ominous sound when she parks behind me.

I'm itching to ask her some questions, but restrain myself for both our sakes. I introduce her to the spare room, glad I keep it made up for Tom's family's visits. As I show her around, I can see her relaxing, and I wonder what she was worried about.

CHAPTER 11

Loretta not only brings a coffee cake, but she offers to stay and scramble up some eggs when Caroline gets up. I jump on the offer, not only thinking of my stomach, but of the advantage of having Loretta around to ask a few pertinent questions. We drink a pot of coffee and I'm beginning to wonder if I'm going to have to roust out Caroline so we have time to eat before we get ready for the funeral.

When Caroline comes in, she is already dressed, in the same thing she wore last night. In the light of day, it's not so fine as it seemed. The collar is worn, and the skirt is a lighter color of black than the jacket, as if it has been washed more often. I'm of two minds about Caroline. I'm mad at her for leaving Dora Lee and not coming back even when her sister, Julie, died. But Caroline has not fared so well herself, and my thinking is that for someone to pull away so sharply, she must have reasons I don't know a thing about.

Loretta bustles around scrambling eggs while I sit with Caroline. I try to think of a neutral question, so I ask her how she likes Houston after being in California so long.

"It's not so bad, but I got used to the weather in California. Houston's hot." You can't get much more neutral than that.

"That's a fact."

Loretta has her back to us at the stove. "Samuel says you got married a while back. You still working?"

Caroline has been stirring her coffee for a full minute now, and it ought to be pretty stirred up. She stops and takes a sip, closing her eyes. "Yes, I'm working."

Loretta scrapes eggs into a bowl and sets them on the table. She unties her apron and hangs it up before she sits down.

"This is real nice. Thank you, Loretta." I pass the bowl to Caroline. "Eggs?"

Caroline takes the bowl, but looks at the eggs with narrowed eyes, as if they might be a trick. "Thank you. I really appreciate your going to the trouble." I notice that her voice is crisper when she says something to Loretta than it is when she talks to me. She takes about a tablespoon of eggs before passing them back.

In normal circumstances Loretta would insist that Caroline help herself to more eggs, but she pretends not to notice and slices the coffee cake. "Hand me your plate, and I'll give you a piece," she says.

Caroline hands her plate over, and when it arrives back, eyes the big slice of coffeecake with the same suspicion she did the eggs. I want to say, "It isn't going to bite you," but I take a cue from Loretta and keep my mouth shut.

"It was a nice turn-out for the visitation last night," Loretta says.

Going from there, we make the smallest possible talk, ending up with not a damn thing being said that puts me any closer to knowing what Caroline Parjeter Wells is up to.

Caroline says she'd prefer to drive herself to the funeral and I tell Loretta I'll pick her up at ten thirty. I'm ready by nine thirty so that I can take a quick side trip to find out the answer to something that has been bothering me.

Our local veterinarian, Doc England, has his business on the same property as his house, south of town. As soon as I stop my truck outside the plain, square clinic, I hear dogs barking inside. The doc is in the pen to one side of the building, bent over feeling a horse's leg. I walk over and stand while he and the horse's owner confer. When they're done,

Doc England comes over and greets me. "Let's go inside out of this heat. You're going to drop dead in that suit."

Inside I tell him what I'm after.

"Yeah, that was a shame. Dora Lee brought that dog in here last week in bad shape. Not a thing I could do."

"What was wrong with the dog?"

"I didn't do an autopsy, but I'm pretty sure somebody poisoned it. She said it was sort of a barking dog, and some people just won't put up with that."

"Anything else could have killed it? Maybe got into something?"

"I asked her if she had any antifreeze around or any snail bait, or rat poison, something like that. But she said no. Poison's the only thing that made sense."

I thank him and get on my way, thinking on my way home about the kind of person who would deprive poor Dora Lee of her dog before he killed her.

Loretta surprises me by being right on time. She wants to get a look at the strangers coming for the funeral. And there are enough to keep everybody busy with the greetings. I shake hands with various first and second cousins. When Greg's Aunt Patsy arrives with her posse, she stops the show. To make sure everybody knows how religious she is, Patsy marches right up to the coffin and in a loud voice says, "Oh, Jesus, take your loyal servant, Dora Lee Parjeter. We are just sheep in your flock." She goes on in that vein for some minutes, while everybody freezes, wondering if they should be bowing their heads or pretending not to listen. Her husband, a skinny man with a thin head of hair, keeps up a steady stream of "amens" as she goes on. After she's done with her conversation with the Lord, she gathers her family around with her and they all bow their heads over Dora Lee. She has five kids, ranging in age from four to twelve, and every one of them stiff as boards and looking like they're scared to death they're going to make a mistake.

After that display, I'm relieved at the low-key service the Reverend Harold Duckworth gives Dora Lee. Although I hear "hmphs" a time or two, I hear a lot more "amens," and by and large everyone seems satisfied that he gets it mostly right in giving Dora Lee a proper Baptist send-off.

In the interest of not inducing heat stroke in the attendees, most of the service takes place inside, leaving just a few words to be spoken at the graveside. Harold Duckworth has sense enough to go along with that, and by twelve thirty we are all back in the Baptist Church fellowship room, where the Baptist ladies have put out a spread so people can eat and talk.

I'm hungry, and the ladies like to see people appreciate what they've taken trouble to provide, so I pile my plate high with pimiento cheese and bologna sandwich triangles, potato salad, coleslaw, and olives. I'm partial to lime Jell-O salad and put a little of that on my plate, too.

The first person to zero in on me is Jenny Sandstone. With that flame-colored hair, she looks good in dark slacks and a white blouse. "You gotten anywhere figuring out what happened to Dora Lee?" I didn't know she was capable of speaking quietly.

I tell her I've come up with nothing concrete, but I'm working on a couple of things. I agree to stop by her place this evening to fill her in.

I then have a chance to agree with all and sundry that the service was very fine, that Dora Lee looked completely natural, and that this is the hottest day so far. Today I don't rush to rescue Caroline, having realized that she needs a little wearing down by people who won't cut her as much slack as I do. Then maybe she'll be a little more forthcoming.

Greg is the object of a lot of attention, Ida Ruth having done an expert job of tipping opinion in his favor. I go over and say hello. Up close, he's a little wild-eyed and he tells me he'll be glad when this is over. "But Grandma would have liked to see all these people turn out," he says. I expect he's heard so many people say that by now that he's adopted it for his own thought, and being able to parrot it keeps him from bolting out of here.

Finally I see who I'm really looking for, Wayne Jackson and his stepdaddy. They have aligned themselves with Patsy and her bunch. I get rid of my empty paper plate, take a deep breath, and prepare to wade in.

Today I notice that although Wayne Jackson and Leslie Parjeter aren't blood-related, they both wear the same discontented expression. I shake their hands, and then do the same with Patsy and her husband. The little ones surprise me by sticking out their hands to shake as well, glancing to their mamma for approval.

Patsy assures me that Dora Lee is with the Lord, using a lot more words than seem necessary. Her husband and kids slip in the occasional "amen." After Patsy winds down, I tell Leslie Parjeter that I appreciate his sending his stepson to get me out from under the burden of dealing with Dora Lee's affairs. "Dora Lee was a long-time friend to me, but it seemed right that family should be there."

"It wasn't me that had that idea. It was Wayne, here."

"Now Daddy, you're the one who called me," Jackson says.

"And I'm sure it was your idea."

Patsy makes her mouth into a smile, but her eyes are uncharitable. I'm wondering if she thinks these two are going to get their hands on something they aren't entitled to. None of these folks stand to inherit a dime, but families are peculiar about guarding rights they don't even have.

"Your folks couldn't come?" I say to Patsy.

"Poor things," Patsy says. "They wanted to come so bad, but they're just too old. It would like to have killed them."

"It's nice that you made the trip," I say to Parjeter.

"Cost me a good bit in gasoline," he says, "But I thought I ought to spare that for Dora Lee."

"Have you met Dora Lee's grandson, Greg?" I say to Parjeter.

He says he has. At the mention of Greg, Patsy purses her lips in that way religious people have of showing disapproval.

"Patsy, you all ought to go out to Dora Lee's after this and get him to show you some of his paintings," I say. "He's got some talent. Have you seen them?" I ask Jackson and Parjeter.

"No, I can't say as I have," the old man says. "I'm sure doing them paintings is fine for them that has rich relatives, but with Dora Lee gone, that boy's going to have to get them ideas out of his head and find some kind of work. His making pictures ain't going to put bread on the table."

"It's true, most artists never make much of a living," I say. "But I know a little about art, and he might be one of those who does all right."

When I say I know something about art, all of them look at me like I had just admitted I keep goats in my living room. A wondrous thing to behold, but of a different order of human.

Jackson says, "How do you come to know anything about art?" Me being a hick small-town old boy.

I tell him that my wife taught me an appreciation for it. "That's why I took note of Greg. You know anything about art yourself?" I say.

He shakes his head. "Not a thing."

Patsy can't keep her judgment to herself any longer. "The Ten Commandments tell us not to have any graven image," she says. "And that means it's an idle pastime to be painting pictures. An abomination to the Lord."

That's the first I've heard of such an interpretation and I don't quite know what to say. More than ever, I'm glad Greg didn't go and live with his daddy's sister. "Was your brother as religious as you are?" I ask.

"No, it's only since Ken and I married that we've seen the light," she says. "I'm afraid my brother was lost to me even before the Lord took him. I wish my nephew had lived with us instead of Dora Lee. We could have set him on the path to righteousness."

After that, as quick as I can I excuse myself and step away from them. I feel a release in my neck muscles. Across the room Rodell is making some middle-aged women giggle. I go over and stand by until he runs out of steam, and then tell him I need to talk to him. The shit-eating grin he's been using on the ladies vanishes. We walk off a little ways, and he squares up facing me with his hands on his hips and his legs planted wide.

"What is it I can do for you?" he says.

I ask him if he's had time to find out if any of his men had word of a strange car out by Dora Lee's.

"I don't understand why this information would concern you," he says.

"It concerns me because I want to see whoever killed Dora Lee brought to justice, and I don't perceive a lot of activity in that direction." I put a little steel in my voice.

"Well, *Chief*, just because you don't *perceive* what's going on don't mean nothing is. Since you was Chief, we've got more technical ways of looking into things."

"I've yet to see any technical thing that takes the place of good, solid footwork."

He looks around the room and from the flush of his face, I believe if we were alone, he might haul off and punch me. "I don't need any so-called footwork to tell me that grandson of hers is guilty as sin. If you hadn't interfered, I'd have him off in Bobtail right now and everybody would be satisfied."

"What evidence do you have against him?"

"That would be in the category of none of your goddamn business," he says.

Rodell's drinking buddy, Carl White, sidles up and tells Rodell it's time they left, and Rodell is more than ready to get away from me. He claps his hat on his head and walks away without another word to me. I'm satisfied that I gave him fair warning. If he's not going to put muscle into investigating Dora Lee's death, then I am.

I go over to where Caroline and Maddie Hicks seem to have run out of things to say to each other. Maddie is trying to hush a toddler in her arms who's about had enough of the proceedings. As soon as I walk up, Maddie excuses herself and hauls the child off to find its mother.

"Have you had a chance to say hello to your Uncle Leslie and Aunt Patsy?" I say.

"Get me out of here," Caroline says. There's a sheen of perspiration on her top lip.

"You've got it," I say. "Put a smile on your face."

As I propel her toward the door, I'm saying nonsense to her to make it look like we are having a conversation. I wouldn't say the set of her lips would be called a smile, exactly, but it tends in that direction anyway.

Outside, I tuck her into my truck. "We'll come back later and get your vehicle," I say. She nods and stares out the front window. "I'll be right back."

I go back inside and thank the Baptist ladies for a fine reception and put some bills into their kitty to help defray expenses. I also press a check into the Reverend Duckworth's hand, pretty sure no one else would have thought of it. And to tell the truth, I didn't either; it was Ernest Landau, the funeral director, who reminded me.

Then I tell Ida Ruth and Loretta that Caroline has had enough and I'm taking her to my place to rest, but that Caroline especially wanted to thank them for all they did.

"That's real friendly of her," Ida Ruth says, with a tinge of sarcasm in her voice that tells me she doesn't believe Caroline said any such thing. Loretta tells me that she'll see me later, one of those proprietary comments she's given to.

As I'm leaving, I notice that Wayne Jackson is talking to Frances Underwood and a man I take to be her husband, Clyde. Clyde is doing the talking, gesturing with his hands wide, and Jackson is nodding. What comes to my mind is the words, "flim flam man." Not something you hear these days, but it seems about right.

CHAPTER 12

I t's about 115 degrees inside the truck. Caroline is looking pale. I tell her to keep the windows rolled down because the air-conditioning has long since given up.

Back at my place, I tell Caroline she should go to her room and get rested up, that I've got some sun tea brewing on the back porch and I'll bring her a glass. "You want sweet tea, or not?"

She unbuttons her jacket and slips out of it. Under it, her sheer blouse is tight against her breasts, leaving not too much to the imagination. Her glance at me lingers longer than seems necessary. "I'll have whatever you're having," she says.

I take my time, giving myself a chance to pull my thoughts together and her a few minutes to get settled in. I bring the big jar of sun tea in and take the teabags out, and I set it on the table. I see there's a message on my machine, so I listen to it.

"Samuel, I got a little information for you," DeWitt says. "I'm not sure what good it will do you. An old boy I know over in Bobtail says he's pretty sure they've tested most everything around there and they've found no new natural gas deposits. He says since the Barnett find up north, everybody's been praying to find a big area like that down in central Texas, but nothing has come of it. I've still got some feelers out, but that's all I know so far."

That figures. Jarrett County, along with its neighbors, has missed out by thirty miles in every direction on oil. And it looks like we've dodged natural gas as well. This has always been a poor area; just a few steps shy of depression. It's land like this—hard to farm, unyielding, tending to drought—that has made men like Leslie Parjeter miserly, begrudging every dollar they spend. They know that they're only one dry season away from ruin. They hold on year after year, but it takes all the joy out of them. I may not particularly like Parjeter, but I understand him.

The only thing that keeps us a little more prosperous in Jarrett Creek is the big lake that the state of Texas engineered about thirty years ago to the west of town. The lake is the reason there is no more creek in Jarrett Creek. Since it was put in, we get lots of boaters and campers and fishermen from all over, and business is pretty good. Before the lake was dredged, the area where it sits was all swampland, good for nothing but snakes, possums, bugs, and quicksand.

With DeWitt's news, I'm back to square one wondering what Clyde Underwood is up to. I've half a mind to get down to the bank right now and ask Gary Dellmore what makes Dora Lee's property suddenly so interesting. But I'm kidding myself. Dellmore is a banker through and through. If he knows something, he's not only keeping it to himself, but he's working as hard as he can to get the bank in on it, along with a tidy little portion for himself.

After ten minutes, I take a glass of iced tea in for Caroline, along with some lemon cookies I keep around, being partial to them.

She has put on a sleeveless blouse and slacks and has fluffed her hair different from the way it was this morning, so it looks softer. It's a lighter brown than Dora Lee's was, almost blonde. She's sitting in the one chair in the room, an uncomfortable old wingback chair I have put there for people to sit in while they put on their shoes. Her hands clutch the arms of the chair as if she's afraid it might lift off and get airborne.

"Thought you might want to lie down," I say.

"Would you like that?" she says.

It's a strange question that embarrasses me in a way I'm not quite ready for. "I don't have any opinion one way or the other. You suit yourself."

I start to sit down on the bed, but instead I go into the dining room and bring back one of the chairs from there. "We need to talk," I say.

"You're going to have to decide what to do with your mamma's land and her things. You and Greg."

She's watching me. "I haven't quite figured out what you are getting out of being involved in Mother's business," she says. She hasn't touched the tea.

"Your mamma and I knew each other for a lot of years. She helped me out when Jeanne was dying, and afterwards. The least I can do is see to it that her death doesn't lead to conclusions she wouldn't have wanted."

"I suppose you think I ought to apologize for leaving here and cutting off ties with my mother," she says.

"I didn't have that in mind." The person I think Caroline ought to apologize to can't hear her anymore. It wouldn't be right for me to tell her I don't give a damn what she does, but right now that's what comes to me. She seems all snarled up in her own self. I don't know what that's about, but she's had thirty years to work it out. If she hasn't done it yet, twenty minutes with me isn't going to change anything.

I take a cookie and offer her one, which she declines. "The business I'm concerned with is your nephew, Greg. He's been dependent on Dora Lee and I know she would want someone to help him sort out the financial end of things."

Caroline reaches over for the tea and sips it. "That tastes good," she says, and smiles a lazy smile.

"About Greg?" I say.

She shrugs. "He's over twenty, isn't he? He can make his own choices."

"You think that way because you were prepared to go out into the world when you were that age. But he's a different person. The boy could be taken advantage of. For starters, Leslie Parjeter wants him as a hired hand without pay. I wouldn't be surprised if Wayne Jackson went along with it."

"You've got that right. That whole Parjeter family . . ." Her voice trails off. I haven't been looking straight at her, and when I do, I'm shocked by the expression of loathing on her face.

As soon as she knows I'm looking at her, she passes a hand over her face and like some magician, puts her expression back into neutral.

"When you were talking last night, I noticed you didn't think too highly of Jackson. What have you got against him?"

She runs a finger over her lower lip. I'm coming to the realization that she has an unconscious way of making all her gestures seem sexual. "Nothing really. Kid stuff. We didn't see them often, but when we did, it had to be us going over to their farm in Dimebox. Mother said Leslie Parjeter was too cheap to ever come to our place. Since I was in Wayne's territory, he always had the upper hand. He tricked me into all kinds of things."

She shudders and wrinkles her nose like she smells something awful. "I guess you know a farm has a lot of booby traps. I remember once Wayne told me their chickens laid eggs in odd places, and he told me if I put my hand down into a box out in the barn, I'd find some eggs. I believed him, and what I got was a handful of chicken shit. Leslie saved it for fertilizer. God, I hated Wayne!" She suddenly laughs, and I see the pretty woman she could be. "He's probably a perfectly nice man, but I guess I know how to hold a grudge."

"Sounds like you've got a reason."

She gets up and glides over to the window. "I take it from what you've said that Mother didn't leave a will."

"I didn't find one, and if Wayne Jackson did, he didn't share that information with me."

Caroline keeps her back to me, looking out the window as she says, "I don't know anything about Texas inheritance law. Do Greg and I inherit equally? Or is it just me?"

"If I'm not mistaken," I say, "kids inherit equally, and if one has died, like your sister Julie, then her half goes to her son. But I hate to tell you, there's not much of anything to inherit anyway."

She turns around. "Really? The farm isn't worth anything?"

"The problem is, before your daddy died, there were big medical expenses and the farm went into a lot of debt. Your mamma paid back some of it, but it's still got a heavy mortgage to pay off."

She sneers, and her voice is hoarse. "Why am I not surprised? They say you can't take it with you, but if anybody could it would be Teague Parjeter."

"I guess he couldn't help that he was sick."

She's moving her hands restlessly up and down her bare arms. "I guess not."

I lean forward with my hands on my knees. "There is one thing about Dora Lee's land, though. It might be worth more than I think." I tell her about Clyde Underwood's low-ball offer and my curiosity about why the land might be more attractive than it would appear. "Could be that Underwood knows something about it that will push up the price. Then you and Greg might get something more out of it."

"I appreciate your looking into it," she says. "I have to tell you, all I really want to do is to sell that land and never look back."

"Why do you hate it so much?" I feel like by asking the question, I'm walking toward a wild animal, hand outstretched to help gentle it. And I may get my hand bitten off for my trouble.

She walks back and picks up her tea and takes it to the window. She sips it and looks out. I wait, sensing that she's almost lured into telling me. But I can also sense when she backs away and slips back into the brush. "One of the reasons I didn't want to come back here is I didn't want to answer any questions about the past."

"That's all right. I thought maybe it would ease your mind to talk about it."

"I don't think so. But about the land, I suppose you're right, I ought to get everything I can from it. God knows, I've made a mess of everything else." She stares down into her glass.

"You got married not too long ago," I say. "I notice you don't wear a ring. What happened?"

"You could say the marriage just didn't take." She sits down on the edge of the bed. "You could also say that most men are out for what they can get. He took me for what little I had. I waited all those years to get married, and thought I had some sense. But it turns out I'm not any smarter than my mother was."

I sit up. "I don't like hearing you talk about your mamma that way, or yourself either. Everybody makes mistakes."

She sits back down and slips off her shoes and runs a hand from her foot, up her shin and back down. "Yes, everybody makes mistakes. Some are bigger than others."

"Just don't throw away an opportunity to make what you can out of the land. For Greg's sake, too."

"You're a sweet man, Samuel. I hope Greg is worth your trouble."

I tell her that I hope so too, and that I think he's a boy with talent.

"I noticed your paintings. I've never been much for art myself. But I remember your wife liked it. This stuff you have is real?"

I'm not sure why I hedge my answer. "It's things Jeanne and I both liked that we bought."

She gestures to a print on the wall above the dresser. "You think Greg could make a living doing paintings like that?"

It's the continual bane of the serious artist, this question. Can you make a living at it?

"Yes, I do. I could be wrong. Plenty of good artists never manage to make a name for themselves, or they go wrong somewhere. But he should at least have the chance."

She sighs. "I'll go out to the farm and see what Wayne is up to. I think that whole swarm of relatives had planned to stop by before they go home." She turns liquid eyes to me. "I don't suppose you can come with me?"

I get up. "I've got one or two things I ought to see about. It's best if you face the lions by yourself."

I don't say so, but I can't help thinking that it will do her good to face off the family with a winning hand behind her. After all, the land belongs to her. And something tells me that when it comes to Wayne Jackson and Leslie Parjeter, she's going to need a backbone made of steel. I tell her I'll run her over to the church to pick up her car, but she says she'll walk over there. "It's just a few blocks."

"You still remember the way out to the farm?"

Her face goes hard. "How could I forget?"

It's late afternoon and I'm suddenly restless. It has been a harrowing day. I'm happy to walk down to where the cows are. They low their greetings, and that soothes me. I walk among them, automatically checking them for anything unusual. Before long I'll have to think about which ones to give up to auction, which ones to breed next spring. But for now I'm content just to be with them.

When I get back to the house, Loretta has been there. She has left a note on the table along with a few slices of cake. Then I remember that I told Jenny Sandstone I'd see her this evening.

I start to call and tell her I can't make it, but then it occurs to me that Jenny may be able to find out something about Dora Lee's land. That perks me up enough to call her, and she tells me to come on over.

CHAPTER 13

"**I**f you can't guess, I'm not much of a cook," Jenny says.

She stands flustered at a pristine counter in her gleaming kitchen, trying to arrange a few pieces of cheese on a plate so that they don't look like mangled chunks of plastic.

"Jenny, I appreciate your going to the trouble, but I didn't come over here to eat. The Baptist ladies took care of my appetite this afternoon. Here, let me do that."

It's strange to me to see a perfectly competent woman be all paws when it comes to food. I move her aside, pile the cheese on one side of the plate and some crackers out of the box she has sitting on the counter on the other.

We sit at the kitchen table where she has already opened a bottle of red wine and put out two glasses. With some women I might be thinking, *Uh, oh,* but I get none of the hints I usually get from a woman who is looking to rope me in. It's more like she was going to have some cheese and crackers herself, and I happened to come by.

I have never been in Jenny's house. I like the way she has done it up. It's comfortable without being fussy the way some single women get. No little glass figurines to catch dust, no smell of potpourri to smother you. The living room she led me through on the way to the kitchen is furnished with a big comfortable sofa and chairs, a handsome rug over polished floors, and a long bookcase full of books. The workings of someone with quiet taste who knows when to stop. On her walls she has a couple of nicely framed art gallery posters and a woven rug. Nothing to get excited about either way, but a welcome change in a town where a picture of Aunt Nelly looking stern or Jesus minding the flock tend to be the wall decoration of choice.

She pours the wine and I sip it. I'm not much of a drinker, a little beer here and there, but the wine is good and I tell her so.

"I like good wine," she says, holding her glass up to the light. "I buy it off the internet. They ship it right here so I don't have to run around finding it and hauling it home."

"Jenny, growing up in Bobtail, how come you moved to a small place like Jarrett Creek?"

She twirls the stem of her glass, smiling a little. "I always liked Jarrett Creek. My daddy used to come over to Granger's Feed Store when he was still farming, and he'd bring me with him. I know it sounds funny, but people always seemed to be a little more modern here than in Bobtail. Even though Bobtail is bigger, it's stuck in the last century. My mamma always said folks here in Jarrett Creek thought they were up to something. Above themselves, if you know what I mean."

"You could have gone to Houston or Austin. A lawyer can make a fine living there."

She laughs, a big cheerful sound. "That's what people say, but the truth is those places are overrun with lawyers. You can make a good bit of money, but expenses are high and I'm just not a big city kind of girl. In case you haven't noticed, I don't exactly have the build for fashion, and I knew early on that I probably wasn't going to be one for marrying."

"Jarrett Creek is lucky to have you," I say.

She pours herself a little more wine and says, "Help yourself when you want more. Now, tell me if you've found out anything about that poor woman's death."

"I wish I could tell you I had, but there's not much to go on. " I admit to my failure in not taking seriously Dora Lee's fear about the car she saw parked out in front of her place the night she died. And about poor old Skeeter being poisoned. "Whoever did it wanted Skeeter out of the way."

"Pure meanness," Jenny says.

I tell her about walking the land to see if there's any sign of oil or gas. We have a laugh over Leslie Parjeter's interest in the possibility, and about him and Jackson circling the wagons to be sure I don't run off with any goods. I wind up talking about Clyde Underwood's low-ball offer for Dora Lee's land. "I wonder if you might be able to find out if there's anything special about that land," I say. "You know people over in Bobtail at the courthouse. They may have some news."

Jenny is looking off into the distance. "I'm trying to think what I heard recently. It seemed crazy to me, so I didn't hold it in my mind."

I sip the good red wine and eat a piece of cheese while she ponders. She slaps her hands together and then points at me. "A race track."

"Horse racing?"

"Oh, good heavens, no. That, I'd have remembered. I mean like a Nascar track. You know, car racing. Some Houston outfit is thinking it might appeal to people around here."

I picture the dust rising from cars tearing around a track out there in the pastureland, a big parking lot with hotdog and beer stands and bleachers—and money pouring into the county. I don't know a thing about car racing, but it doesn't seem crazy to imagine that land being useful for such a venture. "I guess they figure if people come here for the lake, they'll come here for car racing, too. I wonder what kind of money car race tracks bring in?"

"I'm trying to think who I heard it from. It'll come to me and I'll call and see what they know."

"With what you're telling me, I think it's probably time for me to have a talk with Clyde Underwood."

"Lord, I hate to think somebody would kill that old woman for her land."

"Greed makes people do terrible things," I say. "But I'm thinking Underwood wouldn't have had to kill her to get that land. He could have offered her a little more to get her to go along with selling the place."

"People get funny about land," she says. "Maybe he'd had a conversation with Dora Lee, and she had turned him down flat."

"Could be. I know nothing about Underwood. Maybe he's all kinds of crooked. Might be a good thing for me to go to San Antonio and nose around, find out what he was up to."

Jenny smirks at me. "See, I knew you'd be the man to do this investigating."

"Well, I haven't gotten anywhere yet."

Then I go into telling her a little bit about Caroline's past. She watches me, her eyes calculating.

"She's a good-looking woman," Jenny says. "Maybe got used to a better life, and now she's down and out. What's the chances she asked her mamma for help and when Dora Lee turned her down, she got mad and used a knife on her?"

I squirm a little. I don't like the idea that Caroline might have done that to her own mamma, but I can't rule it out. Something runs deep in Caroline that I haven't begun to work out. But all I say is, "I'll have to think about that."

Jenny has been on social time with me, and all of a sudden she's got the eagle-eyed lawyer look about her. "She's the kind of woman that can blind a man to her shenanigans."

I rear back. "I'm a pretty good judge of character."

"I'm just saying what I know from a woman's standpoint. A certain kind of woman says things and does things that another woman sees right off are tricky. But if you tell a man what you sense, the man wants to protect her. That's what Caroline's like."

I remember Maddie Hicks saying how wild Caroline was back in the day, and I recognize how quick I've been to protect Caroline from the women of Jarrett Creek and even from her own relatives. And although I don't really want to admit it, I also think about Caroline's seductive ways. "I'll take that under advisement. Could be you're right. That doesn't mean she killed her mamma."

Jenny cocks an eyebrow at me and shakes her head, in that way women have of saying, "Men! What can you do with them?"

We have a laugh over it. We gossip a little about the Baptist ladies, who are always generous with their funeral spread, but who expect to make a little money for the church for their trouble.

I walk back over to my house and am surprised to see that Caroline's car is not back. It's ten o'clock and I can't imagine what she's got to talk to the Parjeters about so late. For a second I imagine her lying dead out there, the Parjeters having swarmed on her like *Lord of the Flies*.

Inside, I start to get undressed, and then in a stroke of insight, I know exactly where to find Caroline. I sit on the side of the bed with my boots off. I rub my feet. They don't want to go back into the boots, and I want to get into bed. But neither of us is going to get our way.

At night the Two Dog looks better than it does in the daytime, because the shine from the blue neon lights hides the shabby parts. But it still doesn't look good. The building sags on one side, making it look like a heavy wind could tip it over.

I park my truck next to Caroline's beat-up car and heave myself out. My boots crunch on the gravel that's scattered over the hard-packed ground. Two other cars are here, one of them Rodell's. I pause at the door, thinking about what Jenny said about men protecting a certain kind of woman, and wonder if I should just leave Caroline here.

Inside, a stranger is sitting on one of the stools watching Caroline, who is in a clench doing a slow dance with Rodell. His hand is gripping Caroline's butt, pulling her close in. The song on the jukebox is a country-and-western number I never heard before.

The stranger is most likely on the road between Houston and Austin. There's no good direct route between the two cities, and the highway that runs through Jarrett Creek is as good as any other for getting back and forth. Oscar keeps the Two Dog solvent on money from men who stop here to fortify themselves for the final run to one of the two cities. This traveler is enjoying the show Caroline and Rodell are putting on, looking like a hound with a bitch close by. His eyes are little and his mouth slack. I go over and park myself on the stool next to him and ask Oscar for a beer.

Oscar looks at me like I've got a two-headed snake on my shoulder. He's not used to me coming in here much, and especially not late at night. "Samuel, what brings you out this time of night?" he says.

"Couldn't sleep," I say.

"I hear that," Oscar says.

The stranger looks over at me and winks, and then turns back to watch the show.

Caroline has seen me and she looks me in the eye for a second before closing her eyes and continuing the dance. I take a sip of the beer and it tastes awful after the wine I've had. I can't even begin to justify to myself why I came in here, but I suppose I'll have to see it through.

The song ends and Caroline peels herself away from Rodell. He wipes his mouth and anybody can see he's hard from grinding up next to her. He leans down and whispers something in her ear, grinning. She turns toward the bar and walks away from him, and his face darkens.

"I'll have another drink," she says. Without looking over at me, she says, "Hello, Samuel. I wouldn't have taken you for a man who'd drink here."

"Just passing the time," I say.

Oscar hands her a drink that has a cherry in it. I'm surprised he has any cherries back behind the bar, much less knows how to make a drink with one in it. Caroline takes a sip and then eases over to me, coming closer than I feel comfortable with. She puts her hand on my thigh. "I hope you're not checking up on me." On the jukebox another song starts up, some woman with a voice like an alley cat.

It's not like Caroline is a different person than she was this afternoon, but that whatever coiled thing lives just under her skin has been allowed to slither out into the open. She's wearing the same clothes she had on this afternoon, but now I see how tight the pants are and she's unbuttoned a couple of buttons of the blouse so you can see her endowments.

Rodell is watching us. "You here to get some of the action?" he says, his voice mean.

Caroline's face goes white and she puts her drink down on the counter so hard it sloshes over. She doesn't look at Rodell, but closes her eyes. I'm worried she's either going to faint or upchuck.

"Don't get all stirred up," I say. "I just came by to see how Caroline's getting on. She's had a hard day. If you recall, she buried her mamma today."

Some kind of sound like a growl comes out from Caroline and she pushes herself away from the bar and goes back to Rodell. "I want to dance some more," she says. She puts her hands on Rodell's shoulders and molds her body to him.

But his expression has turned nasty. He was thinking that she was a good time in the making, and I've reminded him who she is. He steps back from Caroline, adjusts his pants and looks at his watch. "I better get on home. My wife will be wondering where I am."

Caroline's smile is slow and seductive. "Story of my life," she says. She tries to nestle back into him, but he steps away. He's halfway to the door when the man sitting at the bar, climbs down off his stool and prowls over to Caroline. "I wouldn't mind a dance with you," he says. He puts a hand on her waist and pulls her to him.

"Oh, Lord, deliver me," Oscar sighs. There's no mystery what's coming next.

Rodell stops cold and turns, menace in every inch of his body. "What the hell do you think you're doing?" he says.

Caroline turns to look at Rodell, hair falling over one eye. She giggles and grinds into her new dance partner, who's looking like he swallowed something that didn't taste as good as he thought it would. "The lady said she wanted to dance, and you weren't up to it."

Rodell only gets three steps toward them when Oscar says, "Bar's closing. Rodell, get on home. And you, too, mister. Drink's on the house."

His face twisted with fury, the man pushes Caroline away, pulls out his wallet and throws some bills on the counter. He shoves past Rodell. "Damn two-bit hick town," he says, as he slams out the door.

"You got that right," Rodell says. He follows hard on the man's heels. Oscar comes from around the bar to get outside to make sure nothing more comes of it.

Caroline walks back over to her drink, her steps unsteady. She leans on the bar. "I guess you think now you know who I am," she says.

"It's none of my business," I say. "How did things go out at the farm?"

She still hasn't looked my way. "About what I expected. Between Patsy talking about the Lord and Leslie complaining about the money he's out driving over here, they pretty much took up all the space. And those kids of Patsy's. Reminds me of some movie about aliens. The way they look at you." She shivers.

"What about Wayne Jackson?" I say.

She edges onto the stool next to me. "Oh, he's all right. He's had a chance to get a city shine on him, that's all. He's still the same little boy trying to get on Leslie's good side. He can save his energy."

I wonder how the dynamic between father and son could have been so apparent to Caroline when she was a kid.

Her mouth twists. "I can't wait to get rid of that farm," she says.

Oscar comes back in and sees Caroline sitting next to me. He eyes me with a look I don't care for. I'm not above appreciating a good-looking woman, but it wouldn't sit well if people thought I was after Dora Lee's daughter before Dora Lee was cold in her grave.

Caroline sets her empty glass on the counter and slides off the stool. "Let's get out of here."

"Are you all right to drive?" I ask her when we are outside.

She snickers. "What is it, five minutes to your house? With all the traffic on the road between here and there, I think I can make it." She slips into her car, showing plenty of leg. I follow her to my place.

If I think I'm done with Caroline, I find out pretty soon that she has other ideas. Once we're inside my house, she starts humming, and prances up to me and says, "I'm not ready to go bed yet. You have any music? We could dance." She takes a few steps, jiggling to whatever tune she's hearing in her head.

I suppose I should appreciate that the way her body is moving around stirs me up in a way that I haven't felt in a long time, but I point at my knee and say, "My dancing is limited these days."

"You can watch," she says, her mouth all pouty. She moves closer to me, all the while swaying her hips. Her breasts are inches away from my chest, her cleavage deep and inviting. My heartbeat speeds up and her smile tells me she's heard my breathing get ragged. Despite my best intentions, I reach out and touch her hair. It's as soft as it looks.

"Come on," she whispers. She puts her hand on my chest.

I tear my eyes away, wishing I hadn't drunk the wine at Jenny Sandstone's. I take her hand and move it away from my chest. "You're an attractive woman, no doubt about that." My voice doesn't even sound like my own. "But it's been a long day, and I've got to be up early."

Her smile tightens. "You afraid somebody would find out?"

"I'm pretty sure I wouldn't feel good about myself if things got out of hand."

Her laugh is brittle. "Guess I've lost my touch."

I force a laugh. "I have to disagree. But I have Dora Lee to think about."

Thunder comes over her face and she shrugs and turns away. I'm tempted to take advantage of the mood and ask what it is that was so terrible that it still has a hold on her all these years later. But right now I want to cool things down. "I'll be up and out of here before you get up in the morning," I say.

She mumbles something and walks toward her room.

I let out a breath I didn't even know I was holding onto and head for my bedroom. It takes me some time to get to sleep.

CHAPTER 14

Bobtail High School is a consolidated school that brings in kids from several small towns around it. Its grand, state-of-the-art sports facilities are a contrast to Jarrett Creek's dinky clubhouse. Despite that, Jarrett Creek's ragtag football team consistently trounces Bobtail's team, so the schools have a bitter rivalry.

Even though I've called ahead and made an appointment, the principal keeps me waiting. The secretary tells me he's had an unexpected situation to deal with. Eventually two shame-faced boys shuffle out of his office. It's been a long time since I was in their situation, but I still remember exactly how they feel after being reamed out by the principal.

On the way over, I've plotted how to approach the principal with questions about the art teacher, Alex Eubanks, but I need not have bothered. The principal, a short, trim man with thinning hair, has no compunctions about laying out his opinions. "Eubanks is not the caliber of teacher I want to encourage in my school. I only came in as principal two years ago, and if Eubanks hadn't been here so long, I would have fired him. As it is, I'm trying to find a way to get him to quit."

"How old a man is he?"

"Forty-five. It's not his age that's a problem, it's the fact that he's got a terrible attendance record, and when he's here he doesn't know how to engage the students. He plays favorites and doesn't know a thing about discipline."

"Does he know anything about teaching art?"

The principal narrows his eyes. "A monkey could teach art if he knew something about how to run a classroom. It's not rocket science."

Until he says this, I'm on his side about Eubanks, but now I'm ready to give the art teacher a second chance. "I need to have a word with him. Does he have a free period?"

"Today all his periods are free. He didn't show up—not that that's unusual."

"Is there a way I could get his contact information?"

The principal punches a button on his phone and instructs the secretary to give me what I asked for. I expect he's breaking some privacy law by being so casual with Eubanks's information, but I'm not in a position to complain.

Two cars are parked in the driveway at Eubanks's address, but no one answers the door. Then, just as I turn to leave, a middle-aged woman comes driving up and parks behind one of the other cars. She jumps out and starts hauling out tote bags of art equipment. When I walk toward her, she says, "Are you new? The class is at Alex's studio around back."

I help her with her bags and follow her around the side of the house to the backyard, where a low, rectangular building takes up most of the yard. A sign outside reads, *Alexander Eubanks Art Studio.*

At the door, the woman looks me up and down. "Where are your supplies?"

"I'm just here to talk to Mr. Eubanks. You take classes from him?"

"Oh, yes, I've been taking his watercolor class for over a year. He's a wonderful teacher." She lowers her voice and says, "A little strange, but very encouraging." From the look of the painting that's sticking up out of one of the tote bags, she needs a good bit of encouragement.

The studio is a big space with tables and easels. Eight middle-aged people are setting up to work, with no teacher in sight. The walls are hung with a hodgepodge of work from watercolors to acrylics; from bluebonnets, cows, and cactus, to slashes of color that are probably supposed to represent abstract art. I'm inspecting one of the watercolors, with good workmanship but no imagination, when a man says, "Can I help you?"

Eubanks is a sight to behold. A short man, his sandy hair stands out at least six inches from his head like a wire brush. He wears big round glasses with green frames that make him look like an owl. He's got on a black T-shirt advertising his studio, and baggy shorts show off hairy, bowed legs.

I introduce myself and tell him I want to consult with him about something. "I can see you're busy. I can come back later."

"Consult with me about my work?"

"Partly. It's about a youngster you taught art classes to, Greg Marcus."

He looks suddenly wary, and glances around, as if worried we'll be overheard. "What about him?"

"Like I said, I could come back later."

"Wait outside. Let me get my class started. Then we can talk." His speech is rapid fire.

Standing outside the classroom, I hear Eubanks reel off instructions to the class. I wonder what the principal would say if he knew the art instructor had blatantly taken the day off to teach a workshop.

Eventually Eubanks comes outside. "Now what is it you want to talk about?" There's an aggressive tone to his question.

"I'm a friend of Greg's family. I guess you heard that Greg's grandmother was killed last week?"

"Terrible thing." He knits his brow. "What's that got to do with me?"

"I understand Greg took lessons from you for a while."

"For two years. Then he quit. I guess he didn't have what it takes to be a true artist. I haven't seen him in several months."

"You don't think he had talent?"

"Not as much as he thought he had. He was a cocky boy."

"You were a good teacher. I see from his painting that's he's learned some solid basics. But I understand the reason he quit was that his grandmother couldn't pay for lessons anymore."

Eubanks hesitates. "That's what she said."

"You didn't believe her?"

His smile is beginning to show strain. "She could have found the money if she wanted to. She had a mind to control Greg. Thought I was putting ideas in his head."

"What kind of ideas?"

"Going off to art school. But he had that notion on his own. He was ambitious. If anything, I tried to discourage him. I figured I could teach him what he needed to know."

"Greg told me you came out to the farm and tried to persuade Dora Lee to let him keep taking lessons."

Eubanks cocks his head at me. "Why are you asking me these questions? You think I went out there and killed her because I lost a student?"

"I'm just trying to find out a little bit about what happened between you."

He steps closer and thrusts his chin out, having to look up at me. "If you're looking for who killed Dora Lee, you ought to look a little closer to home. I believe that grandson of hers would do just about anything to get ahead."

"You mean you think he might have killed her?"

Eubanks scowls. "I wouldn't want to guess. Now if you'll excuse me, I need to get back to my students."

Strong words that leave me no doubt that Eubanks nurses a left-over grudge. But I'm still not sure why a teacher would be so angry that someone stopped taking lessons. Angry enough to suggest the boy was so ambitious that he killed his grandmother.

On one side of Eubanks's studio is another room with a sign that reads, *Gallery*. On impulse I go in. I'd like to see what it is Eubanks thinks he could teach Greg.

It doesn't take me long to see that Greg was right; Eubanks is a second-rate painter, with good enough skills but no pizzazz. He paints perfectly respectable pictures of Texas scenes. He uses light well enough, but his composition is off. And there's nothing that takes the breath away, like the first time I saw Greg's work. Who knows what trick of the mind directs an artist to make something fresh and new? Whatever that trick is, Greg has it and Eubanks doesn't. Where Greg has an instinct for where a line of color needs to go to highlight the subtle colors on either side, and draw the eye in an unexpected direction, Eubanks's placement is predictable. I'm wondering if Eubanks even knows that his is the lesser work. And if he does, how it must have eaten at him to see Greg move beyond his ability to teach him anything.

Jarrett County is located in the middle of a triangle that makes it one and a half hours' drive from three Texas cities: Houston, Austin, and San Antonio. Of the three, Houston is by far the biggest, a sprawling octopus of a city on the coast, with different personalities for every section of the city. The oil money there has bought elegance and culture along with sprawl. It's the only one of the three with a sense of humor.

Austin is the capital, and takes itself way too seriously between the government honchos and the oversized university. But it has hammered out a lively world of music for itself. Music has muscled aside the government and the university to give Austin a personality you wouldn't have imagined if you'd been there thirty years ago.

I like San Antonio the least of the three. Not that it is without its attractions. The strong Mexican culture gives it some spice, and it is certainly a modern city. But it carries with it a kind of seediness that it can't seem to shake. It doesn't help that the mayor was recently caught with his hand in the jar. Happens so often all over the country that it hardly causes a ripple anymore. But this one was close to home.

I've left Eubanks's place by midmorning, and despite the snake's nest that they call freeways in San Antonio, I'm at city hall a little after noon. I go to the license bureau and ask to see the archives. A nice lady sets me down at a computer and proudly announces that it's all there. I know how to use a computer, but I'm not adept and she has to get me to the right place. Which, in the end, tells me that Clyde and Frances Underwood had a business license as "City Realty and Development" for twenty years. I look up the big real estate and development offices in San Antonio and leave with some names.

I head for the biggest one, Crane and Company Real Estate. My driving up in a pickup isn't going to give a thrill of anticipation to whoever waits on me. They're looking for somebody who drives a big old SUV or a Cadillac, somebody whose car and clothes scream, "I'm here to make you all some money."

But the agent who greets me, Sherry Rich, acts like she couldn't be happier to fix me up with coffee and sit me down in a comfortable chair. I hate to disappoint her and tell her so.

She has a nice, friendly laugh. "Don't you worry about that one bit. I work on the idea that when somebody comes in here, if they like my style, they'll remember me. One of these days, you'll know somebody who needs a good real estate lady in these parts, and you'll pull out my card. Now what can I do for you?"

"I'll tell you outright, I'm looking for gossip, good or bad. There's a man named Clyde Underwood and his wife, Frances, who ran a real estate business called City Real Estate and Development a few years back. I need somebody to tell me what they can about the outfit."

If I weren't paying attention, I wouldn't see the little flicker in her eyes, because her smile never falters. "Let me see," she says. "City Real Estate and Development was big here at one time. I'm trying to remember what happened that made them pull out of San Antonio. Let me go talk to somebody."

She's gone a good long while, and I use the time to nose around, seeing what is for sale in the Jarrett Creek area. I didn't know that old man Hruska was giving up and selling his farm. Not that it necessarily means anything, but the farm is not far from Dora Lee's place.

Sherry Rich comes back with a man in tow who looks like a businessman with a purpose. He sticks out a big, beefy hand and invites me into his office. Sherry presses her card into my hand and says, "Remember what I said."

Cole Martin is the man's name. He's about twice my weight and a couple inches shorter, which gives him a splendid girth. He settles himself back in his chair and licks his lips like he's about to partake of a fine meal. "You're wanting to know about Mr. Clyde Underwood, and I'm going to tell you straight off we used to call him Mr. Clyde Underhanded." He has a good laugh at his wit, and I laugh, too. It tickles me when somebody is pleased with his own humor.

"Can you tell me anything specific he did that gave him that name?"

He sobers right up. "He and that skinny wife of his made a business of finding folks who were desperate and needed to sell, and giving them pennies on the dollar. Now, I'll tell you what, I'm as ready as the next person to make a fair return out of a deal. But there's a point where I draw the line."

"How would they do that, give them less than a place was worth?"

"I'll tell you how. If somebody comes to me and says, 'I got to sell my place right now, I'm broke,' I'll put it on the market and try to get everything I can for him. It's not just me being a good person, you understand, it's the real estate law. You're bound by your license to get the best price you can for people. Well Underwood made a practice of offering somebody a low-ball price right there in his office. He'd buy the property, then turn around and sell it for a tidy profit."

"So that's what he was up to," I say.

Martin slaps his desk. "I'll tell you more, too. Not only would he buy it himself, at under-market, but he'd also charge them his usual broker's fee. Insult to injury."

"Couldn't the law do anything about it?"

He leans forward. "It's a problem if you can't get somebody to take him to court. These people he beat out didn't have money for a lawyer, so they were stuck with the deal. People like Underwood give all us legitimate real estate folks a bad name, and we were glad to see the back of him."

"What happened to make him get out?"

"Went one step too far, as any crook will do."

"Can you tell me a little more about that?"

"Hold on. Let me get us a soft drink. What can I get you?"

I tell him I could drink another cup of coffee.

I can see why this outfit is one of the biggest. They earn their money the hard way—by taking time even with somebody who doesn't come in with ready cash.

When Martin comes back he says, "It turns out that when Underwood put things back on the market, he would start rumors, saying something big was going to happen around the property. That would drive the price up."

"You mean like starting a rumor that an outfit was interested in building a car racing track, to get the land value driven up?"

"That's exactly right. I was on the real estate board at the time, and we were itching to catch him at it. Finally he made the mistake of putting one of his rumors in writing to somebody who knew a thing or two. Next thing you know, he and his wife are closing up shop and slinking out of town."

"Never did jail time?"

"The real estate board had the evidence, but we figured it wasn't worth our time and money to chase them down. They were gone, and that was the important thing."

"I want to ask you one more thing. It's of a little more sensitive nature. Was there ever any idea that Underwood might go to an extreme to get a hold of some property?"

Martin blinks a couple of times. "How do you mean extreme?"

"Like roughing somebody up, or even more than that."

His eyebrows reach his hairline. "Like murdering somebody? Well,

I never heard of that. I think he was sleazy, but I never heard of him being violent."

I get up, put my hat on and give him my hand. "I can't thank you enough. This is just the information I needed."

"I take it you're not asking out of idle curiosity?"

"The Underwoods have landed out in my neck of the woods. I can't prove anything, but I think they're up to something. What you've told me gives me information I can zero in on."

"You a lawman?"

"Concerned citizen," I say.

"Well, good luck. You keep us in mind if you know somebody who's looking to do business in these parts."

CHAPTER 15

When I roll up to my place in the late afternoon, I'm relieved to see that Caroline's car is gone. I'm wondering if I would have been more of a fool last night if Jenny Sandstone hadn't warned me about Caroline.

The mail I've been letting accumulate on the front table nudges me, so I get myself a glass of tea and some lemon cookies and sit down on the porch to go through it. It's still blistering hot out here, but after being in the city, I feel like sitting outside. It smells good in high summer, the scent of honeysuckle so thick in the air it could almost knock you out.

The mail doesn't amount to much—a few bills, a couple of cattle auction ads, and a couple of notices for Houston art gallery openings. I set the notices of the openings aside to think about later. I haven't bought any art since Jeanne died. My heart hasn't been in it.

The phone rings. When I'm outside I often let it ring, but with the irons I've got in the fire, I feel the need to answer it. As soon as I hear Loretta's voice, I feel guilty. I've been neglecting her, and there's no call for that. She may be pushy, but she's a good woman and I see no need to give her an unhappy time.

"Loretta, I'm glad to hear from you." I tell her what I was up to this morning. "If you have time, come on down here and have a glass of tea with me."

"Is Caroline there?" she asks. I know she has heard about Caroline's performance at the Two Dog last night and my part in it.

"No, I don't know where she's got off to. Probably out at Dora Lee's."

"I'm surprised you're not keeping closer tabs on her."

"Loretta, are you coming down here or not? Or wait, I'll tell you what. Let me take you out to a nice dinner tonight. We could go over to Frenchy's." I'm not partial to French food, but Loretta likes it.

"I don't know whether I ought to. Ida Ruth and I are going out to Elgin tomorrow morning to look at headstones for Dora's grave. Her grandson said he'd be glad for us to do that. We thought we'd get an early start." Her voice is so full of regret that I know she wants to be persuaded.

"Come on, Loretta. We'll go over there early and get on back so you can get to bed at a reasonable time. You could order you some of those oysters you like."

"Samuel, August is not oyster season," she says. "But I could get some crawfish etouffe."

She can't see me make a face. I can't imagine how anybody can eat a critter like a crawfish with all those little prickly tentacles. "All right, then. I'll come by about six o'clock."

I've got a little time, so I head on over to the jail to talk to whoever is on duty. Even though Rodell would resist my asking questions, I can pretty much count on him not being there so late in the day.

Over at the jail, James Harley is startled when I walk in. He shoves something into the desk drawer real quick, but not before I see that he's been entertaining himself with a titty magazine.

"What is it you want?" he says. He's surly and I don't know if it's because I interrupted his session with the magazine or if he got into trouble with Rodell for not putting up more of a fight when I got Greg out of jail.

I set down the sack I've got with me and pull out two of the beers I brought, figuring I might need a bribe. "I need you to help me out with something," I say. I pull up a chair and sit down with a foot crossed over my knee.

The beer lightens his attitude considerably. He takes a long pull. "Nice and cold." He sets it down and belches softly. "All right, shoot."

"Before Dora Lee was killed, she told me she saw somebody in a fancy car sitting out on the road in front of her house. I'm wondering if there were any rumors of somebody seeing an unusual car out there in the last couple of weeks."

James Harley takes another long swig. He props his boots up on the desk and folds his hands over his stomach, and says he has to think about it. I can almost hear the wheels creaking as they turn in his brain. Finally he swings his feet to the floor and goes over to the file cabinet. "I'm going to say it was Earl told me something about that." He ruffles through what I take to be incident reports. "Here it is. And it was Earl. Says here it was weekend before last there was some boys drag racing over at the dam."

I wait for him to tell me the connection between drag racing at the dam and seeing a car out at Dora Lee's five miles away, but finally I have to ask.

"Earl said he got to talking with the boys and they told him they saw some foreign sports car when they passed by Dora Lee's on their way out to the dam."

"Did Earl tell you who the boys were?"

He gestures toward the file cabinet. "It's all right there. We keep good records. It was the Armstrong twins and Jack Kunkel."

The Armstrong twins. I'd as soon try to get information out of an alligator than out of an Armstrong. That family has been raising up hellions as long as I can remember. I went to school with Robert Armstrong, and there wasn't any boy in school that didn't feel his fist or his boots. And when I was the law around here, they were always up to no good. The thing is, the Armstrongs waste all their energy on striking out at the world around them, leaving nothing left over for honest hard

135

work. No telling how those boys have come by a car they can race up on the dam.

I thank James Harley for his information, and before the door is closed behind me, I hear him opening the desk drawer.

The Armstrongs live on the hard-luck side of town. I'm not surprised when I pull up in front of their tin-sided shack to be rushed by a couple of nasty dogs. I tell them to get back, and they're so surprised that somebody would speak sharply to them that they settle right down and follow me through the maze of torn-apart cars squatting in the yard.

Cathy Armstrong comes to the door. She's a big, tough country woman. Her gray hair is pulled back in a fierce bun at her neck. I'd hate to see her with her hair flowing free. "Samuel Craddock, what brings you over here?" Her voice is not unwelcoming, the way it would have been if I were still a lawman.

"Cathy, it's good to see you again. You doing okay?"

She says she's poorly with her back, but other than that she's fine.

"I'd like a chance to have a word with your boys. They might have some information that could help me out."

"Information about what?"

"You know Dora Lee Parjeter, the woman who got killed at Cotton Hill?"

"I've seen her a time or two." The welcome is gone from her voice. "My boys didn't have nothing to do with that. They're good boys."

I wave my hands vigorously. "No, no, don't get me wrong. It's nothing to do with them. I just hear that they saw a car out at Dora Lee's that they took notice of, and I'd like to see if they can tell me something about that."

"Well, I don't know." She's looking for the hitch in my story. "Come on in. Let me see if they can talk to you."

"Why don't I just wait out here? I don't want to keep you from your business."

"Suit yourself." She disappears back into the house.

After a few minutes identical teenaged hulks come tumbling out the front door, hitching up their pants and grinning to each other. They've got big flat faces, eyes set close together, and hair that I imagine their mamma cuts.

I stick out my hand, and they shake with me, both turning red in the same degree. I gesture to the cars scattered out front. "I notice you all take an interest in cars."

"Yessir, we sure do," one of them says.

"Which Armstrong are you?" I say. "I swear I never saw two people look so much alike."

They snicker as if they've never heard it before. "I'm Cecil and this is Felix."

"Cecil, I understand you noticed a fine car parked out at Dora Lee Parjeter's place sometime in the last couple of weeks."

Cecil grins. "We sure did. I'd like to get my hands on a car like that."

"What can you tell me about the car and if you can remember when it was you saw it out there."

"It was a ragtop," the one called Felix says. "A foreign make. Smallish, like a little sports car."

"Yessir, that would be one hell of car to drive," Cecil says.

"Did you see it once? Twice?"

"Two times. Both times it was parked down near the road, not up at the house."

"Did you see who was in it?"

The two boys squint at each other in an effort to recall. "It was a man," Cecil says, "but we didn't pay any attention. Being that we didn't know the car, we didn't figure we'd know who was driving it."

"Big man? Small?"

"I guess we would have noticed if he had been outsize, one way or another. He wasn't shrunk down behind the wheel, but I didn't notice him being real big."

"Any idea what nights he was out there?"

They look at each other and shrug. I'm liking these two boys. They're not shy about talking to me, but they're not smartasses or surly either. Being twins, maybe they feel a little more secure in their ability to take care of themselves than some of the other men in their family.

Technically they were breaking the law by drag racing at the dam, but they're just boys, glad to be out of school for the summer, roaming the roads at night like boys have been doing since I was a youngster, stirring up whatever they can to use up time and energy.

"Did you see the car out there last Thursday night?" The night Dora Lee was killed.

They exchange looks again. "We wouldn't have seen it that night even if it had been there, because we were over visiting somebody in Bobtail." Cecil punches his brother on the arm, which tells me they were in Bobtail to see some girl.

"In case you were to see that car again, could you do me the favor of getting a license plate number?" They say they'll be glad to. I thank them for their time, and then I have an idea. "You two boys need any work?" I say. "I could use some help at my place."

They have twin looks of regret. "We appreciate it, but we've got a job over in Bobtail, working for a garage. We work over there every day, from morning until two thirty."

"You must be pretty good at this stuff," I say.

Hands on his hips, Cecil surveys the yard. "We've been at it since we was twelve," he says. He points to the one car that looks intact. "That's how we got our car there. We put it together from some junkyard cars that daddy hauled out here. It can get up to some fair speed."

"You all be careful," I say. They look at me and grin the way boys do when they think nothing will ever happen to them. But I know it can, remembering a couple of incidents that I'd prefer not to have been a party to, pulling mangled bodies out of fast cars, when I was chief of police.

When I get back to my house, Caroline's car is still not back and I begin to wonder if she has gone on back to Houston without telling me. I take a look in the spare bedroom, and sure enough her things are gone. She's left a note propped up on the bedside table. *Samuel, I've moved out to the farm for tonight. Thank you for your hospitality. —C.* I'm thinking she must have some sense of shame about last night to move out to the farm, as much as she hates it.

I go out and sit on the porch and run through my mind the things I've learned today and how they fit with Dora Lee's murder. Why would she have thought somebody was after her? Surely Dora Lee would have told me if someone threatened her. But maybe she wouldn't have if it was her daughter. I try to imagine Caroline threatening Dora Lee, but even though Caroline has an edge to her, it's hard for me to be serious about her making a threat. One thing is certain, something sent Caroline out of that house thirty years ago and she's never really gotten over it. I'm thinking maybe I'll have to make another pass at talking to Maddie Hicks.

My thoughts turn to the car the boys described today. I let my imagination loose. Could the Underwoods have hired someone to spook Dora Lee into selling her place and it got out of hand? Could the fancy car belong to Caroline and she borrowed a friend's heap to drive here? Maybe Wayne Jackson has a second car to complement his big SUV. Or maybe the car belongs to somebody who hasn't even come into the picture yet.

139

CHAPTER 16

So Loretta will approve of the way I'm decked out to go to Frenchy's, I put on some black pants and a light blue shirt with a black string tie, and I'm pretty pleased with myself when I walk out the door.

Loretta takes her time. That's why I told her I'd pick her up at six o'clock. I figured by the time we got over to Frenchy's it would be close to seven. When Loretta finally makes her appearance, all tight-curled and wearing a crisp yellow and white dress, I've become acquainted with all the articles in her new *Good Housekeeping* magazine and don't feel better informed for it. I ask Loretta if she'd rather I drive her car than my truck, so we can arrive in style, and she likes the idea. She has a nice little Chevrolet, and its air-conditioning works, which on a hot August night is a blessing.

At Frenchy's I stick to ordering what I know; steak and a baked potato. Loretta orders the special, which she always does, since she likes to be adventuresome in her eating. I start to order a beer, but then remember how nice that wine went down at Jenny's, so I ask if I can get a glass of red wine.

"I never knew you to order any red wine," Loretta says.

I almost tell her I had some at Jenny Sandstone's last night, but think better of it. "I was just thinking that at a French restaurant, wine might be the thing. You want some?"

She shudders and makes a prissy face. "Ice tea is just fine for me." I suspect Loretta would like a glass of wine if she'd ever tried it, but her husband was a rigid teetotaler, and she went along with him.

Talk starts out well between us, with us going over details of the funeral and the reception. Loretta has all kinds of news to impart that

I was not privy to. Things like who is in the family way; whose son has decided not to go off to college after all, making his mamma cry with happiness and his daddy mad at the lost opportunity; who is sick; who has gotten better. All the things that run through a small town and make you appreciate the ebb and flow of life, even if you don't know much about the people involved. Loretta keeps peering at me when she thinks I'm not looking, and I know she's thinking about what happened at the Two Dog last night.

I figure the best defense is a good offense. "I had me a problem last night."

"What problem?" she says.

"Dora Lee's daughter went off to the Two Dog and had herself a little too much to drink and I thought I better go get her out of there."

The dam breaks. "Well, I don't know why it had to fall to you to take care of somebody like that. She's a grown woman. I hear she was making up to Rodell, and he's a married man. I hear they were practically going at it on the dance floor. How come you had to get involved? It's not like you and Dora Lee . . ." She stops abruptly, having gone one step too far.

"Dora Lee was a good friend, and Caroline was staying at my house, so I felt some obligation."

Loretta's cheeks are bright pink. "I don't understand that to begin with. She could just as well have stayed out at Dora Lee's farm."

I'm wondering how I'm going to ease her off the subject, but I remember what Jenny said about the kind of woman Caroline is, and I figure that deep down Loretta has the same instinct for Caroline that Jenny does, and I won't get past it. So I just say, "With all those Parjeters out there at the farm, I thought she might need some privacy. And it worked out all right in the end. She was just a little stirred up by the funeral."

I couldn't have asked for a better time for our food to be served. It puts us back on a good footing, and after a few bites, Loretta says, "How long do you figure Caroline is going to linger here?"

"She said something about having to get back to work. Loretta, I know she's a strange kind of woman, but I believe life hasn't been all that kind to her, and it won't hurt for people to let her alone."

"If she'll leave us alone, we'll leave her alone." Loretta dabs her lips with her napkin.

"I don't think she wants to be here, but she's got to do something about the property."

Loretta suddenly gets a smirk on her face, and she reaches up and pats her hair.

"What are you so smug about?" I say.

"I just know something you might not know," she says. "I stopped by Frances Underwood's place this morning to get some eggs, and she told me something interesting."

It makes me embarrassed for Loretta that Frances Underwood is going to use her to spread the rumor that Dora Lee's property might amount to something. If I had Frances Underwood here right now, I'd have plenty to say to her.

"Well, tell me what she said."

"She made me swear not to tell."

"All right, then. I wouldn't want you to go back on your word."

She takes a couple of bites of her dinner, and I say something about how nice the wine is and how nice it is to sometimes come to a place that has white tablecloths. I'm about to say how nice it is that everybody dresses up a little to come here, when she says, "Well, I don't suppose it would hurt if I told you. She just meant don't spread it to all and sundry."

"Whatever you think is best."

She peers at me to see if I'm being sarcastic, but decides I'm not. "Some big outfit from Houston is thinking about putting a race track out there."

"A horse racetrack?" I ask, all innocence.

"No, a car racetrack. They think people who come to the lake will come to the car races, too."

"I thought Underwood wanted to farm that land."

"I asked her about that," Loretta says. "She's a kind of woman I think knows more than she lets on. She says that's exactly what they were going to do, but then they heard about this racetrack some time back and decided it might be best to see what came of it, before they put in the time and effort to bring the land up to where it could grow crops."

After that, we discuss what a big change it would be to have racing out there. She says there'd be people for it and people against it, and I agree. We wind up the evening on friendly terms.

In Jarrett Creek we're headed toward our part of town when I see flashing lights up ahead, like an ambulance. I wonder if it's for old Mrs. Summerville next door.

"What in the world?" Loretta says. "Look at the sky, there's smoke." Anxiety clouds her voice.

I have a sudden feeling of dread. It's as hot a night as we've had, and I wonder if something has caught fire. We turn on to our street, and I yell out, "Oh, my God!" The fire trucks are sitting outside my house.

I hit the accelerator, and come to a screeching halt at Jenny Sandstone's house, because I can't get any closer. Jenny is out front with Elvin Crown, head of the volunteer fire department.

I leap out of the car and rush toward my house, as fast as I can go with my knee hitching up.

"Whoa, whoa!" Elvin says and he almost tackles me from behind. "You can't go up there just yet."

"My paintings," I gasp. My heart is pounding so hard, I feel faint. Jenny is at my side and takes hold of my arm. "It's okay. Your paintings got out of there."

"Are you sure? How?"

"The volunteer boys and I got them out."

I bend over for a minute with my hands on my knees to get my bearings and feel Jenny holding onto my arm. "I'll be all right," I say.

"You had a bad scare," Jenny says.

I straighten back up and now that my head is cleared I can see that the house looks intact, although the smell of smoke is strong in the air. Loretta has gone over to talk to neighbors who are in a huddle across the street, taking in the action. I'm surprised to find that Rodell is here, too, looking somber. I ask Elvin for the details.

"You have Jenny to thank," Elvin says. "If she hadn't seen it, the whole house would have gone up."

I look at Jenny full on and see that her hair has gotten loose and is wild around her head. There are smudges of soot on her face and on her Houston Astros T-shirt.

"You shouldn't have risked your life," I say.

"It wasn't like that," she says. "It had barely started when I got to it. By pure luck I was down watering my horses and I saw some light through the trees. I thought it was coming from the back of your house, but then I realized it was flickering, and it didn't look right. So I cut up through your back yard and I saw right away you had a fire at your place."

I tense up again with the thought of what could have happened. "And you got the art out of there."

"I didn't see your truck out front, so I ran back to my house and called the fire department. I knew you had all those paintings in there, so I went in and started bringing them out. These volunteer boys got here in nothing flat. They chased me out, put some water on the fire in the back and got the rest of the art out."

Elvin is standing there nodding as she talks. "If she hadn't called us when she did, the whole place would have gone up," he repeats. "As it is, the walls at the back are blistered and you've got some water damage and some smoke inside."

"I'm afraid I broke down your front door," Jenny says.

Loretta has come back and is hovering nearby. "Oh, my Lord," she moans.

I guess the relief of knowing everything is all right makes me giddy because I start laughing right out loud.

"What's so funny?" Elvin says.

I finally wind down and wipe my eyes. "I don't lock my door. Jenny, you could have just walked in."

The look on her face gets me laughing again until everybody catches on, and we're all snickering like fools.

"I don't know how I can thank you enough. Those paintings mean everything to me."

And I don't mean only their monetary value. They represent a tie to Jeanne and a world that we made together. I may not be able to thank Jenny properly, but I know one thing: Jenny won't ever have to go down there to water those horses again.

CHAPTER 17

I awake in a strange bed, disoriented for a minute and feeling anxious, my heart doing a little overtime jittering. Several times in the night I half-woke, and don't feel that I've really been all the way asleep. The smell of coffee brings one or two synapses back into play and I swing my legs off the bed. My whole body feels sore, as if I've run too far, the aftermath of an adrenaline rush from last night. I take a deep breath and remind myself that my paintings are safe and that according to Elvin the house is intact. What I want to know is how the fire got started. Figuring that out is just one of the things I need to get busy with.

The bedroom I'm in has the same quiet but comfortable feel as the rest of Jenny Sandstone's house. Last night she took charge of me, brushing past my protest that I could just as well stay in my house. "It's going to smell of smoke. Tomorrow you can air it out, but tonight you don't need to sleep with that smell." I went into the house long enough to get my shaving apparatus and a change of clothes.

Jenny's spare bedroom has its own bathroom, so I feel like I'm in my own cocoon. I go in and take a shower, which takes some of the edge off my itchy mood.

"I figured you'd be up early," Jenny says. She's already dressed for the day, moving around briskly and making me feel ancient.

"Never was one for lying in bed."

She sets a cup of coffee on the counter in front of me. "This is as far as my breakfast hospitality goes. I've got a meeting in Bobtail this morning, so I'm on my way. Make yourself at home. I don't know what kind of breakfast you eat, but you might find an egg or two and some cereal."

Then she's gone in a whirl of briefcase and purse and perfume.

In spite of my abundant dinner last night, I'm hollow this morning, so I scramble Jenny's last two eggs and toast the last two pieces of bread, and make a mental note to restock her larder. While I eat, I look through the pictures Jenny retrieved from my place. She has them stacked neatly in her living room in a corner near the bookcase. Seen altogether this way, I realize how many I have. My hands shake as I touch the first one, unable to hold back thoughts of what could have been if Jenny hadn't been down there watering her horses.

I get the Wolf Kahn out and hold it in my hands for several minutes. There's not a one of these pictures that I don't know exactly where Jeanne and I were when we bought it. I notice the glass is sooty, so I pull out my handkerchief and wipe it off. I'm going to have to call an expert in to see if any of them have been damaged, or need to be professionally cleaned.

The phone ringing breaks my reverie. Thinking it may be presumptuous to answer Jenny's phone, I almost leave it, but then think it might be her calling about something. It's Loretta, checking in to make sure I survived the night. She offered for me to stay at her place, but her notions of propriety are strong, and I could tell her heart wasn't in it. Jenny seemed to sense the same thing, and she insisted I'd want to be where I could check out my paintings first thing in the morning.

I tell Loretta I slept fine and she says I can count on her to help with anything I need.

I could spend the whole day looking at those paintings and celebrating the fact that they are intact, but I need to go over to take a look at my place and figure out what to do about the damage. And I've got something else to do first.

Leaving Jenny's, I walk around back of my house and down to the pasture where the tank is. The cows come crowding around, as if they know something unusual happened last night. "Ladies and gentlemen, get ready to welcome some strangers."

I walk over to the fence between Jenny's place and mine, to the gate that hasn't been opened since she moved in. The gate has settled and is hard to open, but finally it gives enough so I can slide the handle sideways. The gate swings open and I pull it all the way back to the fence.

Jenny's three horses are standing together near the fence, watching me as if they've never seen a man before. I walk toward them gingerly, but they hold their ground. If they had spooked, I would have, too. "You're welcome to come through any time," I say. But then I realize that my cows are going to come in here and eat up all Jenny's grass, so I go back and close the gate. Jenny and I will work out the details later. But at least the gate has been opened once and it will get easier.

Coming back up to my house from the pasture, I'm greeted by a sad sight. The back of the house is blackened and peeling. Again, I wonder how the fire started, and I don't like the way my thoughts tend.

Nothing at the back of the house would make a fire spark spontaneously. If it had started in the kitchen, it would have taken a while for it to blister the back walls the way it has. I have a bad feeling that this wasn't an accident. Somebody set it, starting it around back so it would have a good chance to consume the place before anyone would notice it. The plan just failed to take Jenny into account.

I'm trying to settle my mind around the idea that somebody would do something so destructive when I hear a grumpy meow. I turn around to see Zelda stomping toward the back door, where her food dish usually sits. The fire has charred the dish and the steps it sat on. People who don't know cats may not think they can stomp, but Zelda can. She's mad as hell about the disruption in her life.

"Let me go inside and I'll get you a new dish," I tell her. She honors that idea by finding a place on her side that needs some heavy grooming.

The floor is gritty and my boots crunch as I walk through the house to the kitchen, at the back. The paint is peeling off the cabinets from the heat of the fire, and the whole room is gray with soot. I open the cabinet and take out a cereal bowl, fill it with cat food, and start to open the back door, but the handle is seared, and won't budge. I take the bowl back through the front door and around the side and set it down in the grass near the blackened steps. Zelda walks over to it, stiff-legged and suspicious, but decides to go along with my new plan.

When I get back around front, Elvin is just pulling up. He's a barber in town as well as being head of the volunteer fire department, and he's here early so he can get on to work. He stands with his hands on his hips, his baseball hat tipped back on his head, and looks at the untouched front of the house. "You got yourself some luck," he says. "Jesus was on your side last night."

"Jesus and Jenny."

He chuckles, but sobers right back up. "I need to talk to you about something," he says.

"I know what you're going to say. Somebody set this fire."

He looks me full on. "I'm afraid so. I've put in a call to the fire chief over at Bobtail. He wasn't in yet, but I left him a message to call me at the shop. I expect he'll want to come over and see what he can make of it."

"I guess I can't have anybody clean up until then."

"If I was you, I'd call my insurance company. You know, they've got these fellows who come out and investigate a suspicious fire. Might be to your advantage."

"I'm going to take that advice. But I want you to know, I'm going to tell everybody what a first-rate job you and your crew did."

He takes off his hat and dips his head in acknowledgment of the compliment.

When he's gone, I head back inside. Before, when I came in, I had a mission to take care of Zelda, but now I get the full effect of the fire. The smoke smell is strong, so I turn off the air-conditioning and open up the windows. The house seems strange to me without the pictures. I pass by the dining room and see that no one thought to take the Neri sculpture. That would have been a loss. But I remind myself that it *isn't* a loss; it will need careful cleaning to get the soot off it, but it's still here.

I'm suddenly sorry that Loretta had to go off with Ida Ruth today. I would have liked hearing her yoo-hooing me about now.

By now it's close on to eight o'clock, still too early to call the insurance company. But I phone my nephew Tom and tell him what happened.

"I'm coming down there myself right now," he says.

"No, you just go on with your day. I'm fine. It wasn't much damage."

"I can cancel my appointments. I don't like the idea of you having to face that alone."

I calm him down and tell him how I appreciate his concern, but that I'm not really alone; I've got all kinds of people on my side. He makes me promise that I'll call him tonight. If he was my own son, I couldn't feel any more pleased with that boy.

With a little time on my hands, I'm itchy to get back to Jenny's to take a closer look through my pictures to see if there's any damage that needs to be seen to right away. I couldn't quite take it all in first thing, my mind being on getting over here to assess the property. I'll feel better if I satisfy myself.

At Jenny's I pour the last cup of coffee and turn off the pot, then go through the pictures. I have nineteen of them, many of them not particularly noteworthy, a few decent prints and some line drawings. But five of them have turned out to be the kind of investment that art collectors dream about. And one of them, probably the most valuable one, is missing. It's a Wayne Thiebaud cake picture that Jeanne and I bought early on, in San Francisco, a pink and cream confection on a light green background—not one of my favorite paintings, being more Jeanne's taste. But it turns out she was right about the painting's potential; it's worth an indecent amount of money. Before Jeanne died, we put in our will to leave it to the Modern Art Museum of Fort Worth. The firemen couldn't have missed it, because it was right over the fireplace.

Before I panic, I call Jenny to ask if she might have stuck the painting somewhere else. Maybe she even recognized that it might be valuable.

"Thiebaud? I don't know anything about him. But I put all the pictures in the same place. You've had a shock. Maybe you just missed it. I'd go back through them if I were you."

"I'll do that. And Jenny, I'd just as soon you not mention that anything is missing."

Now I know what the fire was about. Somebody came in and took that picture and was willing to destroy all the others to cover up the theft. I'm breathless with fury, so I sit still until I can think properly about who would have done such a thing. And whether it is connected to my investigation of Dora Lee's death.

CHAPTER 18

E lvin said he was going to get the fire investigator from Bobtail involved, and insurance investigators will come out eventually, but I'm too impatient to wait for them to get to it. I want to find out now if any of my neighbors saw somebody hanging around before the fire started.

The obvious place to start is with old Mrs. Summerville next door. In her nineties, Mrs. Summerville is not as spry as she was, so her daughter, Letitia, who lives with her, parks her in the front window of the house everyday so she can see everybody who comes and goes.

Letitia shows me in to talk to her mother, fussing over me as if I were an honored visitor, instead of just the man next door. I guess they don't get a lot of action, and last night my house provided them with enough to talk about for some time to come, so I'm something of a celebrity.

After I'm settled knee to knee with Mrs. Summerville, and she has told me how she and her daughter liked to have had heart attacks when they heard the fire engine stop next door, I tell her that Elvin thinks somebody set the fire.

Her hand goes to her chest and her mouth starts to work as if she's chewing on the information. "Well, I swan," she says, in the old way of saying "I swear." "I never thought of such a thing happening right next door. Did you ever hear of such a thing, Letitia?"

Letitia agrees that she never did.

"What I'm wondering is if either of you saw anybody outside my house yesterday evening after I left."

"You was taking Loretta Singletary somewhere, all dressed up," she says.

"Yes, ma'am, we went over to Frenchy's, that restaurant in Bobtail."

"The French food with all them snails. I don't believe I could eat that."

"Mamma, you told me you saw somebody go to Samuel's door and then walk around back," Letitia says. I'm grateful to her for pulling the conversation back around.

"It was a boy. He was in a reddish kind of a car," she says. "Wine-colored."

"You said it was a Ford." Letitia sounds impatient.

"I don't know anything about cars, but it had that thing on it that Fords have. You know what I'm talking about?"

"The medallion on the front grill?" I say.

"That's it. Medallion. Fancy name for it. I couldn't read it from here, but I know what it looks like."

"Could you describe the boy for me?" I say, although I know she's talking about Dora Lee's car, and there's only one boy who would be driving it. Sure enough, she describes Greg, and my thoughts take a bad turn.

I ask her if she saw anyone else around, but she says after that she and Letitia ate their dinner and watched TV, so they wouldn't have seen anybody.

I make a quick tour of the other neighbors, but get nothing to show for it. Most of them were busy eating dinner or at the TV by early evening.

When I get back to my place, a big red SUV is sitting out front, *Fire Marshal—Bobtail, Texas* printed on the side in yellow letters. My front door is open, so I call out and let the fire marshal know I'm here.

Woodrow Callum is a tall man with skin the color of molasses and the erect posture and close-cropped white hair that suggests a military background. He shakes my hand with a firm grip.

"Mr. Craddock, you've got yourself a situation here," he says in a deep baritone. I like him right off for being direct. "I found it hard to credit when Elvin called and told me he thought this fire was arson, but he was right on. Come on around back and I'll show you."

He has a long stick with him, and when we get around back near the porch, he crouches down and pokes it under the porch to point out a couple of half-melted bottles with charred rags next to them. With my bum leg, I can't squat the way he does, so I have to get on my hands and knees to look at it.

"Unless you find it handy to keep some kerosene and rags under your porch, I think we can assume whoever did this put them there."

"Sounds about right."

Callum pokes at the charred rags. "Well, look at this," he says. With the stick he brings out one of the rags, and it's only party burned, one corner seared, but intact. He brings it closer and points to it. "There's some kind of stamp here. When I get it to my lab, I may be able to make out what it says."

"It looks like whoever did it wasn't particularly sophisticated in their methods. Am I right about that?"

He stands up and gives me a hand up. "I was just going back to my truck to get some bags to put this stuff in. Walk with me and I'll explain a few things."

On the way to his truck, he tells me he took the job as fire marshal in Bobtail to get a little salary to supplement his retirement and to keep busy. "I retired from the army after twenty-five years and then was a fire inspector for an insurance company for another fifteen before my wife and I moved to Bobtail to be near our family."

"So you've seen a few fires," I say.

"Yes, sir. What you said about the person who did this not being sophisticated, is right on. Most people who set fires aren't sophisticated, and this one is about standard. It's been my assessment that people who set fires like this are desperate one way or another. They've got financial problems or a score to settle or they're covering up something, like a theft or even murder. They're not people who've thought out the business of starting the fire. They just use whatever they can pick up. They assume the fire will burn up the evidence. More often than not, that's just plain wrong."

155

He opens the back of the truck and takes out some serious-looking heavy duty plastic bags with thick plastic closures.

"I think I can help out on motive." I tell him about the art, and the one painting missing.

He looks at the pavement as I speak, nodding. "So you figure somebody set the fire to cover up the theft of your picture."

"I'd appreciate it if you'd keep that part quiet. I'll be notifying the insurance company, and no question they're going to send somebody out to investigate. I hope that doesn't step on your toes."

"It depends on who it is. Some of the inspectors I worked with thought they were the last word in smarts. And me being a black man didn't always sit well."

"Even with your experience." I say it as a fact, not a question.

"Even so. I'll give them my cooperation, but I won't lie down and play dead."

"You let me know if you need any backup on my part."

"You ex-military?" he says.

"Just my stint in the air force. A pretty boy just seeing enough to know I wanted to get on back home."

We both laugh.

"I'll let you get on with it," I say. "I have a couple of phone calls I need to make."

The woman I reach at the insurance company is concerned when I tell her about the fire, but she's really upset when I get to the part about the Thiebaud being gone. She asks if I've filed a police report. I tell her I'll get right on that. No reason to tell her that Rodell isn't going to be a whole lot of help. I tell her the fire marshal has been here. She asks me if the painting had an alarm system, and I remind her that I pay an extra premium so I don't have to do such a thing.

She still doesn't like it. "We'll be sending somebody to investigate right away," she says in a crisp voice. "We're going to be right on it. Somebody will call you as soon as we set something up. Is this the number where I can reach you?"

I tell her it is, and to leave a message if I'm not here.

"Can I get your cell phone number?" she says.

"I don't have one," I admit. "We don't get good service here, and most folks don't find it useful to have one."

"Well, where are you?" she says, indignant, sounding like she's pretty sure I have to be calling from another planet.

I tell her we're a small town and she has to make do with that. She says she'll be in touch.

The truth is, I never have figured out why somebody can make a phone call from an airplane or a mountain somewhere, but the mobile phone companies can't make it possible for us to have coverage in Jarrett Creek. Not that I care, particularly, it just strikes me as obstinate on their part.

I see that I have missed a couple of messages. One is Tom's wife, Vicki, pitching a fit about the fire and telling me I ought to come up there for a few days. The other is from Jenny. "I've got something that might interest you. Call me."

I call her, but just get her machine, so I leave a message that I'll be home for a while.

I'm about to starve, so I pull out some lunchmeat and make myself a sandwich. I go around back and ask Callum if he'd like me to make him one, too, but he says he's going to have to get on back to work.

The smell in the house is so bad that I sit out on the porch, and while I eat, I ponder who might have set the fire and stolen my painting. Even though Mrs. Summerfield said she saw Greg at my house, and he certainly needs funds, I can't imagine that he'd be stupid enough to show himself so blatantly and then come back and set fire to the house. Besides, there's no way an artist would burn up those paintings.

Callum was talking about a desperate person setting the fire, and the first name that comes to mind is Caroline. I don't know what it comes from, but she's certainly got an air of desperation about her, something edgy that I can't figure out.

And then I think of Clyde and Frances Underwood. I don't know how desperate they are, but I know they like money. The truth is, I like the idea of the Underwoods being responsible, because I just don't like them. They stuck her mother in a nursing home, rather than making her last days comfortable at home. It would have been easy enough for them to know about my art. They could have heard it from Loretta, or Greg or even Gary Dellmore at the bank. It's not a secret that I have an art collection; it's just that most people don't have much interest in it.

I can't even think about a country boy like Leslie Parjeter in the same universe with a Thiebaud, but greed knows no limits. And Wayne Jackson looks prosperous enough. But looks can be deceiving. It sounds like he owes his daddy some money, and he might have thought stealing my painting was a way to make a bundle.

I don't know how my fire and theft are connected to Dora Lee, but it seems too great a coincidence not to be. With that in mind, I think about my confrontation with Alex Eubanks yesterday. Like with the Underwoods, I don't know how he would have found out I have a valuable art collection, but I do know he has a vindictive turn of mind toward Greg. It wouldn't hurt to find out more about their relationship.

CHAPTER 19

It seems like a long time since I've been out to Dora Lee's, although it was only Sunday when DeWitt and I were here.

Three cars are parked in front: Dora Lee's, Caroline's, and Wayne Jackson's SUV. I'm surprised to see that Jackson is still here. I'd have thought he'd have work to get back to in Houston.

I go around to the back door and can hear the argument way before I reach the house.

"You crazy bitch, you're going to screw things up royally," Wayne yells.

I don't hear the reply, but I'm pretty sure the crazy bitch is Caroline.

I don't knock at the back door, just open it and walk in. I'm interested to find out what the element of surprise will bring me. "Hope I'm not interrupting anything," I say.

Caroline is sitting at the kitchen table clutching a cup of coffee like it's the only thing keeping her from slipping off her chair. Her back is rigid. Jackson is standing over her with his hands on his hips, looking even bigger than he is. His face is dark and sweaty. If I were Caroline, I might even be scared. When she turns at the sound of my voice, her face is pale and haggard.

Jackson glares at me, drawing a hand across his mouth as if to wipe away a bad taste. "What is it you want?"

"I need to talk to Dora Lee's grandson and see how he's doing. I heard voices and thought maybe he'd be in here with you."

"Well, you can see he's not," Jackson says.

"That's a fact," I say. "Caroline, how are you getting on?"

She gets up from the table, pushing herself up with her hands, as if she's stove up. "I'm glad to see you, Samuel." She throws a cold look

159

Jackson's way. "You might be interested in the conversation we've been having."

"Leave him out of it. This is a family thing," Jackson says.

"Wayne wants me to sell my mother's land to Clyde Underwood," she says. "I'm not sure that's such a good idea."

"Underwood is making a fair offer," Jackson says.

"Hold on," I say. "Everybody just calm down. Wayne, if you recall I got a look at what Underwood was offering, and I think Caroline's right, she can do better."

Jackson takes a couple of steps too close to me. "I'm not stupid. I told Underwood his offer was too low, and he came up considerably."

"You mind if I sit down?" I say. "I've had a kind of shock, and I'm a little played out."

Caroline frowns. "What kind of shock?"

I sit down with my shoulders hunched as if I've got a heavy burden, playing it up a little. "Somebody set fire to my house last night."

"Oh, my God!" Caroline says. She brings a hand up to her throat. "You didn't get hurt, did you?"

"No, I'm fine. But I would like to ask you what time you left my place yesterday."

Caroline flushes and doesn't meet my eyes. "I left as soon as I got up, about ten."

"I don't suppose you saw anybody around my place who shouldn't have been there?"

She shakes her head.

"What kind of damage did you have?" Jackson says.

"I'm one lucky son of a bitch," I say, "A neighbor of mine saw the fire before it could get out of hand."

"How do you know somebody set it?" Jackson asks. "It's pretty hot. Maybe you had a little gas leak and it ignited."

"No question it was set deliberately."

Caroline sits down next to me and puts her hand on my arm,

gazing into my face. "Why would anybody do such a thing?" For once, she seems to be outside her usual concern with herself. "What about your art? Is it okay?"

"Damage was just to one wall of the house. And the volunteer fire department got my paintings out." I'm not ready just yet to noise it around that I lost a valuable painting.

"Glad to hear it wasn't too bad," Jackson says. He's looking at me in a thoughtful way. "Any idea who might have done it?"

"Not yet. But the fire investigators will figure it out. The fire marshal in Bobtail is a pretty savvy guy." I don't mention the insurance investigators because I want whoever did this to think it's a small-scale operation.

"Who'd guess so much would go on in a small town?" Jackson says with a smirk. "If I were you, I'd be trying to think who my enemies are."

"I expect it won't come down to me thinking about it too much. The fire marshal told me that arsonists aren't that smart, and usually something trips them up." That's not exactly what Woodrow Callum said, but I want anybody who might have set that fire to be nervous about being caught. And as far as I'm concerned, right now these two are as likely as anybody to have done it.

"I hope he's right," Jackson says.

"Anyway, we were talking about Underwood's offer," I say. "What makes you think it's a good offer?"

Jackson has been standing all this time, and now he sits down, sprawling back in his chair like he owns the place. "Underwood used to be in the real estate business, and he said he knows what things are worth. He said the only reason he made an offer was because he knew Dora Lee had financial problems. He was thinking he'd help her out."

"Uh, huh." I'm nodding as if I accept what he said. "Did he say how he knew Dora Lee had financial problems?"

Jackson swipes at a fly buzzing his head. "I assumed it was common knowledge."

"Maybe." I'm thinking that when I have a spare minute, I'm going to have words with Gary Dellmore down at the bank about his loose talk with people's financial information.

"Caroline, what would you like to do with the land if you don't want to sell to Underwood?"

Caroline looks to Jackson. "She wants to put the property on the market," Jackson says. "I told her she'll be having to pay real estate fees, and by the time the real estate people are done with their negotiations, she'll get less on the open market than she will if she just goes ahead and sells it to Underwood."

I'm wondering why he has a dog in this fight. From the looks of it at the reception after Dora Lee's funeral, he and the Underwoods were doing some negotiating of their own. Could be they've put him in the way of making a little on the side if he convinces Caroline to go along with selling the place.

"The thing is," I say, "I heard a rumor about the land, something about a Houston outfit wanting to put some recreational thing out here. That would up the value of the land considerably. I'm surprised Underwood didn't mention that to you."

Jackson's face has gotten flushed. "Underwood did tell me about that, but he said it's pure speculation. Caroline and Dora Lee's grandson aren't in any position to be speculating." He opens his hands out in appeal. "Caroline, I know you don't believe it, but I've got your best interest at heart."

Caroline's laugh is not a pretty sound. "Wayne, you've never had anyone's interest at heart but your own."

Jackson's mouth turns down in a pout. "You have no reason to say that."

"You're a Parjeter—I know, not by blood, but Leslie raised you, and some of his tight-fisted ways rubbed off on you."

"Leslie was a good daddy to me." Jackson's fists clench up.

"Wayne, don't be a fool. Leslie treated you like a servant. He didn't even go to the trouble to adopt you, because he was too cheap to pay the filing fees."

"He would have done it if he could have afforded it." Jackson's face is getting red again.

"If he was so wonderful, why did you leave there the minute you got a chance?"

They sound like a bickering old married couple that is going over the argument for the hundredth time.

"Listen here," I say. "This isn't getting anybody anywhere. Let's get back to the matter of your selling the land. The plain fact is, Caroline, you can't sell by yourself. You've got to have Greg's consent to whatever you do, because he'll inherit half. Does he have any opinion in the matter?"

Jackson has a sneer on his face. "Not yet. He says he's got to think about it. What the hell does he know about the land?"

"He lived here with his grandma," I say. "I believe that counts for something with him."

"He's going to have a fight with me if he tries to keep it," Caroline says. "The last thing I want is to have this land hanging around my neck."

"You realize that no matter what you decide to do, you won't be able to sell it until the probate of Dora Lee's estate gives you title? That could take a year."

"Underwood says there may be a way to get around that," Jackson says.

My guess is that what Underwood has in mind is to forge Dora Lee's signature on a contract. Wouldn't be the first time, but there's no way I'm going to let that happen.

Caroline looks around the kitchen, her eyes hard. "As long as I can leave here knowing I don't ever have to come back, I don't care how long it takes to sell it. And Greg's going to have to live with that."

"Which reminds me, I actually came out here to talk to Greg." I get up from the table.

"He's gotten to be quite the popular guy," Jackson says. "You're the third person who's been out here to see him."

"I expect people want to pay their respects," I say.

"Didn't look that way. Some little girl came wheeling up yesterday morning in a big SUV that makes mine look like a little sports car. She was a prissy thing, not as cute as she thought she was. I guess she was out there about an hour, and when she left, she laid down about half the rubber on her tires."

He looks over at Caroline and they both grin. "We figured she was out here for a quickie."

I'm put off by their insinuation. But I have to wonder why the girl came to see him. Greg told me he was a loner, so who is the girl? "You said somebody else came by?"

"Some weird, bristle-haired guy. Looked mad enough to hit somebody, too. He didn't stay long."

Walking out back to Greg's cabin, I think about why Alex Eubanks would have come to see him. Greg takes a minute to answer his door, and when he does, he's blinking and he has that faraway look in his eyes, like he's been in his own world. He has a smear of pastel chalk on his face. "Mr. Craddock, I'm glad to see you. Come on in."

My eyes shoot to the easel. He has put aside the painting he was working on when I first came here and has started another one. I don't see how this boy can be contained here in this small part of the world.

"You're working hard," I say.

He looks at the painting and frowns. "I'm going to have to figure out how to get some supplies. I'm running low on a few things."

"We'll figure something out," I say. "Greg, I'll come right out and ask. A neighbor of mine saw somebody that looked like you at my house yesterday. Did you come by?"

He sits down on the bed, his face losing its animation. "Yes, I needed some advice, and I thought maybe I could talk to you."

I clear some rags off his only chair and sit down. "Advice about what?"

"You know Caroline wants to sell this place."

"And what do you think?"

"The more I think about it, the more I don't want to. But I can't stop her because I don't have any money. She's says I'll get half the proceeds, and I have to have something to live on, so I guess I have to sell."

"You like it out here."

"This is where I landed after my folks died, and my grandma was good to me. I have my studio set up here. And it's quiet." He looks off in the distance. "Maybe if I was set up somewhere else, I'd like it just as much, though. As long as I can work."

What draws me to Greg's work is that it has the land in it. Not a landscape, but the expanse of it, and the colors of the soil and the grass and the wild weeds, and the sky with clouds or with sun. I think about Diebenkorn and the series he did that has ocean in it. And Georgia O'Keefe with her passion for the desert. Not that Greg paints like Diebenkorn or O'Keefe, but his work spins up out of this land with the same kind of passion. It wouldn't be a bad idea for him to spend some time in other places, and expand his horizons. But it would be a shame for him to not have his prime territory to come back to, if he wanted.

"Why don't you hold out on making a decision for a few days? There's no hurry, in spite of what Caroline says. Nothing can happen until after probate anyway, and that could take up to a year."

"A year?" He looks panicky. "I don't know what I'm going to do for money. I'm going to have to get me a job, fast. Wayne says maybe he can find something for me."

"Before you go off just getting any old job, I'd like to have somebody I know in Houston take a look at your work. You could bring a few of your paintings along that you feel like you might be ready to part with. While we're there, we can pick you up some supplies."

"I'm not really good enough for anybody to buy my paintings yet. I know that."

"You may have to let me advance you a little bit of money," I say.

"Then when the estate is settled, we can figure out how I can get paid back." What I'm thinking is that I might buy a couple of things from him, but I want George Manning, a gallery owner I know, to take a look at the work first. I don't want to falsely encourage the boy if I'm off track.

"I don't know what to say." His face is a mixture of uncertainty and eagerness. I'm struck by how damned young he is.

"I had a fire at my place last night," I say.

His expression freezes. "A fire? What about your art? Was anything burned?"

It's the right response. I just flat don't believe he would have set that fire. "No. Everything is safe." Again, I see no reason to bring up the Thiebaud.

He blows out a breath of relief. "That would have been like, I don't know, the worst thing I can think of." He looks around his studio, as if imagining his work being burned. "How did it happen?"

"Nobody's sure yet. Could be somebody set the fire."

He jumps up. "Set it? On purpose? What would they do that for?"

"That's a good question. I'm going to leave that to the fire inspector to worry about. Now I need to talk to you about something else. I went off to see your old teacher, Alex Eubanks, yesterday."

Greg shoves his hands in his pockets and rocks back on his heels. "I know. He told me. He came by here yesterday afternoon as mad as a wet hen."

"What was the problem?"

"He seemed to think I said something that made you suspicious of him. I told him I only told you the truth."

"Was it the truth?" I say.

"I don't know what you mean."

"You told me your grandma couldn't pay for lessons, and that you'd outgrown him as a teacher. I think there's more to it."

Greg goes over to his easel and stares at the painting he's begun. I realize the colors are different; some flesh tones and softness. It makes me think of a woman's skin. "I guess you're right," he says.

"Eubanks have a daughter?"

He nods.

"She came out here to see you yesterday. What did she want?"

As if he's on automatic, Greg chooses a color from his pastels and lays a few strokes on the canvas. "Same thing she's always wanted," he says, eyes on his work. "Sex. I don't mean to sound conceited, but she's always been after me. She said she came out to tell me she was sorry about my grandma, but it was just an excuse." He makes a few more strokes, then lays down the pastel and looks at me. "Why me? She could have a lot of guys."

I think about Caroline being so seductive toward me. I've asked myself the same thing. Why me? "I guess it's the age-old question," I laugh a little. "Maybe because you weren't available."

He wipes sweat off his brow with the back of his arm. "It's not like I don't think she's cute." He gestures toward his painting. "But I don't have time to do the things she wants to do. Go out and ride around, go to movies. Even if I did have time, I don't have the money." He picks up another color and starts dabbing at the painting.

"And her daddy got mad because you hurt her feelings?"

Greg pauses and looks at me curiously. "No, he didn't know anything about us. She was always scared he'd find out we were messing around."

"Then he just came out here because he was mad that I came to see him?"

He puts down the chalk and dusts his hands off. "He told me you pretended to be looking at his paintings, but you were just snooping around. I told him he was wrong, that you probably were looking at the art, because you're really interested."

"Did you tell him I had an art collection?"

He puts his hands on his hips, staring at me. "I did. Was it the wrong thing to do?"

"I don't know. I hope not."

CHAPTER 20

When I walk back in my house, my phone is ringing. "Listen to this," Jenny says. "You know that business about the racetrack? Well, it turns out that may be real. I talked to a businessman I've done a little lawyering for, and he told me he thinks that outfit from Houston is serious about buying up several spreads around there."

"Would you happen to know the name of the outfit?"

"Samuel, what kind of lawyer would I be if I didn't get that information for you?"

She tells me it's called "Best Land Use Enterprises."

"Well the name doesn't leave anything to the imagination, does it?"

"You want me to give them a call and find out what I can?"

"Let me try it first." I want to talk to them about the Underwoods in person, which gives me one more reason to head over to Houston.

So now to tackle my main reason to want to go over there. I fish out a card from a gallery that Jeanne and I did a fair amount of business with, the one we bought the Wolf Kahn through and a couple of other pieces. I'm glad to hear that George Manning is still around. The last I knew of it, his son was coming up in the business.

"Oh, yes, I still take an active role," he says, when he hears who is calling. "Art is in my blood. I hope when I drop dead it's in front of a fine painting. But that's not what you're calling to hear. Are you ready to add something to your collection? Or are you out to sell a piece?"

"I wish it was that uncomplicated. I've got two things on my mind." I tell him about the theft of the Thiebaud.

He is suitably outraged about the fire. "That just makes me sick. You've got probably the best Wolf Kahn I ever had my hands on.

169

To think that somebody would willfully destroy it is beyond understanding. And the Thiebaud! Whoever did this must not know much about art. It will be impossible to sell it to a legitimate dealer. Only the most underhanded ones will touch something that unmistakable."

"That's exactly what I'm afraid of. Suppose somebody took it who doesn't know that? If it gets to be too much trouble to find a buyer, I'm afraid they'll do something foolish, like destroying it."

Manning groans. "I hope we're not looking at something like that."

"So my question is, is there some kind of network that you can call into play so potential buyers will be on the lookout for it?"

"I can certainly notify people I know in Texas, but the problem is, whoever stole it could take it out of state and I don't know what happens then. If he gets it to someone unscrupulous, they could have contacts with those who don't care how they get a piece of art. They're willing to pay for it, because they won't ever show it. It will just sit in their vaults."

"I've heard about people like that. The Van Gogh piece that will never see the light of day."

"It's the most famous, but there are others. I'll do what I can to make the alert. Art dealers get their backs up over this kind of thing, so they'll put out the word. Now the problem you have to face is publicity. TV news people will get wind of it right away, and you're likely to be the object of a lot of attention."

I hadn't even thought of that. "I'll have to handle that the best way I can. If you can keep my name out of it, I would appreciate it."

He says he will, and advises that I also call the gallery I bought the piece from out in California. "Their name will be on the back of the painting, so whoever took it might think that's a clever way to sell it."

I think him for the suggestion.

"Now you had something else you wanted to talk to me about?"

"This is a whole different topic. I don't pretend to be good at this, but a young man has come to my attention who looks to me to have some talent."

"You have a very good eye," he says. "Maybe not as discerning as your wife's, rest her soul, but I'll take a look at his work if you think this boy is worth it."

"I do. I happen to have some urgent business in Houston. What if I brought the boy in tomorrow?"

We agree on early afternoon. That means another trip out to Cotton Hill to tell Greg. I don't want to talk to him on the phone about it, because I'm afraid he'll make up some reason why he's not ready. I think it's just as well to get him to Houston fast, so he doesn't have time to brood on what pieces to bring in. If he's like any other beginning artist, he'll just start finding flaws and get himself all worked up.

And while I'm out in Cotton Hill, I believe it's time I put in a visit to Clyde Underwood.

I'm just thinking about whether I ought to phone Woodrow Callum regarding Allen Eubanks, when from the front room I hear my name called. "Samuel." Caroline's voice has a timbre to it that gives me a chill.

CHAPTER 21

"Come on in and sit down," I say, trying for a natural tone, but feeling unaccountably nervous.

Caroline sets her purse on a chair, and walks into the kitchen, toward the table, moving like somebody walking through a bog, and worried about quicksand. I don't smell alcohol coming off her, but her eyes have the glazed look of somebody on a bender. I go over and pull out a chair for her, because it looks like she would have trouble negotiating it. She sits down and crosses her legs. She's wearing a tight skirt and a low-cut shirt.

"Can I get you some ice tea or a cup of coffee?" I say.

She gives a throaty little laugh. "Maybe a little water," she says.

My mouth is dry, so I get water for both of us and sit down across the table from her. She's tracing the lines of plaid on the tablecloth with her finger as if it's the most fascinating design she's ever been up close to.

"To what do I owe the pleasure of this visit?" The words both sound and feel false, but I have to start somewhere.

"I'm on my way back to Houston, and I came by to apologize," she says. "I feel like I owe that much to you."

"You don't owe me anything," I say. The person she owes an apology to is her mamma, but Dora Lee is dead, so she's not going to get the benefit of it anyway.

"I didn't behave very well the other night. It wasn't fair to you, as nice as you've been to me." Her hands are starting to jitter, and she rubs them along her arms.

Suddenly her strange manner comes clear to me. "You're high," I say.

She curls her lip. "You think I could face that farm any other way?"

"I wouldn't know. I don't have the information I'd need to make a judgment on that."

"No, I guess you don't."

"So why don't you tell me?" A bead of sweat rolls down the side of my face, and I dash it away with the back of my hand. I have the windows open, trying to air out the stench, but the heat is so oppressive that I'm wishing I'd closed up the house and put the air-conditioning on.

"You really want to know?"

I nod.

Sweat is glistening at her cleavage, and she plucks the shirt away from her body to get some air. "Everybody in this town looks at me like I'm a monster for leaving here and never seeing my mother again. I tried to make myself come back once or twice. But I couldn't stand it." She lifts her hair off her neck and lets it fall back. "If you all knew what I had to put up with out at that farm, you might be a little more forgiving." She sips her water, and her eyes wander around the room. She winces as she looks at the blistered back kitchen wall, but doesn't say anything about it.

"Caroline, I know your daddy was a violent man."

"You don't know the half of it."

I don't think it takes a genius to figure out what more was going on, but from the pain I see in her eyes, she needs to tell somebody, and it might as well be me.

Her voice turns harsh. "You asked for it, and I'm going to tell you. My daddy started coming to my bed when I was eleven years old. The first few times he kept his hand over my mouth so I wouldn't scream. I thought I was going to suffocate. I learned to keep quiet. I was a child and I believed him when he said it was my fault for being such a sexpot. Those were his words. My own daddy."

"Caroline, I'm so sorry." It makes me sick to think what Teague was up to. You can't live in the world and be ignorant of such things, but you never think it will be someone you know; even someone as low-life as Teague Parjeter.

Caroline draws a shuddering breath, clutching her water glass so hard I'm afraid it will shatter. "He kept it up until I got the courage to leave. Everybody around here said I was wild, but it was the thing he was doing that made me wild."

For a minute I have to look away from her wretched expression. I'm wishing like hell I'd never pushed her to tell me. But I did, so I force myself to face her again. She's watching me with her dark eyes.

The smell of smoke seems stronger in the air than it was, making it hard to breathe. "Wasn't there anybody you could go to? A teacher? The Baptist preacher?"

"Who's going to believe an eleven-year-old girl? You think the preacher would believe me?"

I remember the Baptist preacher from thirty years ago. He was an elderly man, or at least he seemed so at the time, and I can't picture any little girl trying to talk to him, especially about something as big as Caroline's troubles. I shake my head.

"For the longest time, I thought Teague was right, that it was my fault, and by the time I realized he was just a sick, nasty man, I felt too tainted to try to do anything about it. I had to get out of here."

And then I recall something Jeanne said after Caroline left, that sometimes people did what they had to do. "Did Jeanne know anything about this?"

She stops her agitated moving for a minute and thinks hard on the question. "She must have guessed something. I told her I had to get out of here. She said I should tell her before I left and she'd see to it that I had some money. She gave me three thousand dollars and said not to worry about paying it back. That sometimes people just needed a boost, and she was glad she could help me."

I feel the sense of disorientation I always feel when someone tells me something I didn't know about Jeanne, partly jealousy that they got a tiny piece of her I didn't get, partly grateful to have her even stronger in my mind.

"Why didn't you tell your mamma?" I say. "She could have put a stop to it."

She shakes her head wearily. "If only it was that easy. I was afraid. About everything. I wanted to tell Mother. I hoped she would kill him. But then I was afraid she would, and then she'd go to jail. I wanted to run away, but I was scared he'd start on Julie. Julie was always more fragile than me, and I knew it would be the end of her." She ends in an anguished moan. Tears are trickling from the corners of her eyes, leaving twin streaks of mascara. "What could I do? I was a kid."

She stands up and goes into the front room and grabs up her purse. For a second I'm worried she's going to do something violent. I picture her bringing out a gun and shooting me, or herself. But she's after a tissue. She wipes at the smears of mascara around her eyes.

Back in the kitchen, she stands in front of me. "After I left, I began to wonder if Mother knew what was happening. How could she not know?"

"I just don't believe that. I wish to hell you had gone to her. She would have found a way to tell me."

She sits back down, clinging to my words. "Do you really think she would have done something?"

"I do."

We sit quietly for a few minutes. I'm trying to make sense of why Jeanne didn't tell me what she suspected. Was she afraid I'd kill Teague outright? I have mellowed some over the years, but maybe then I would have snapped.

"I need to clear up another thing," Caroline says. "I lied to you about the man I married. He didn't take anything from me. I don't know why I told you that. He tried to fix things for us, tried to be gentle with me." She puts her head in her hands, and her hair cascades around her face. "He pretended he didn't know I slept around behind his back every chance I got. But eventually he gave it up. I don't blame him."

She walks to the refrigerator and pours herself another glass of water. When she turns back, she looks at me for a long time before she speaks. "I thought I'd feel better if I told someone, but I don't. I'm damaged property, no matter what."

"You know it wasn't your fault. You have to find a way to put it behind you."

She moves to my side and puts her hand on the back of my neck and begins to rub it. For a few seconds I let myself go with it, sinking into the sensation of her fingers working my muscles. I imagine how it would feel to put my arm around her waist. She's right next to me. But Jenny's voice pops into my head with the one word, "shenanigans." I put my hand around Caroline's wrist and move it away. And at that moment I wonder if everything she told me was a lie.

She turns away from me so I can't see her face, and says, "I guess I'd better get on home."

I'm wavering on the question of belief in her story, and then I think, what would be the purpose of such a lie? To justify staying away so long? To explain her seductive behavior? I stand up. "Why don't you let me fix you something to eat before you leave?"

"I can't eat anything."

But I make her a sandwich anyway, and while I work, she goes to one of the charred cabinets and touches it. "What a mess," she says. "It smells terrible in here. How can you stand it?"

I tell her I'm staying with a friend.

"You could stay out at the farm. Wayne's gone back to Houston. I'm sure Greg would be glad of the company."

"Maybe I'll do that."

"How long is it going to take before the damage is repaired?"

I set the sandwich down on the table, and she looks at it for a few seconds. There are dark circles under her eyes. Finally she sits down and picks up a half sandwich. I sit down across from her.

"It might take some time. What I didn't tell you and Wayne this morning is that one of my paintings is missing."

"Really. Was it very valuable?"

I nod. "The thing is, that whoever stole it has got a problem on their hands. Nobody can sell that painting."

She almost has the sandwich to her mouth, but stops. "Why not?"

"It's too well-known. No legitimate dealer will touch it. You can't just take it in somewhere and plop it down. They'll call the police right away."

She gives a bitter snort, as close to laughter as she's capable of right now. "Somebody is going to be awfully disappointed." She sets down the half-eaten sandwich.

"Oh, they'll be more than disappointed. The insurance company will be sending out investigators, and they're not going to want to pay the insurance money until they've done everything they can to find whoever took it."

"Well, I hope they do," she says. I'm watching her reaction, and she looks thoughtful, but not worried. Either she's a damn good actress or she had nothing to do with the fire and theft. She gets up and takes her plate to the sink.

"Before you left, did you have a chance to talk to Greg about the property?"

"Yes. I can see he loves that place, but even if I didn't want to sell, I don't see how he can keep it without any money coming in."

"I'll tell you the same thing I told him. Don't rush into anything. Have you thought about a lawyer to handle the probate?"

She walks into the other room and gets her purse. "Wayne said he'd take care of it for me."

"That's nice of him." He must think there will be some advantage to him in keeping control of the situation. "I'm going to recommend somebody to you anyway. She's here in town, and that might be an advantage, since the papers will have to be filed in this county."

I write down Jenny's information and Caroline puts it in her purse.

I tell her she can stay the night and get a fresh start tomorrow, but she says if she's not back at work in the morning, she'll likely lose her job. "I can't afford that." Still she stands there, as if uncertain how to leave.

"Where is it you work?" I say.

"South Houston Savings Bank," she says. "I'm in the computer department."

Being cooped up all day staring at a computer sounds about as boring and depressing a job as I can imagine. "You like it?"

"It pays bills," she says, shrugging. "In this economy, I'm glad to have a job at all."

"You miss California?"

She cocks her head. "I do and I don't. I think coming back to Texas was a mistake in more ways than one. Out in California it seemed easier to keep my mind on my everyday life and not dwell so much on what happened in the past. But maybe it would have been better if I had confronted it earlier."

Suddenly I remember the box of mementos I took from Dora Lee's closet. "Hold on," I say. "I've got something to give you."

I bring the duffle in and set it on the table. "I don't know what you want to do with these, but I think you should be the one to decide."

She puts her hand in and brings out a couple of cards and the clipping about the artist and lets them fall to the table as if they've burned her. "I don't think I want this stuff."

"I'll keep them for you in case you ever change your mind."

She looks at the article. "You could just throw this away."

"You know anything about the artist?"

"My grandmother bought a painting from him when they were living in Austin. I guess he was down and out and sold it to her cheap. My mother said grandma said he would be famous one day."

"What picture is that?"

"It was an old landscape," she says. "I noticed it wasn't in the house. Wayne said he thought she sold it quite a while back."

I walk her to the door, and wait while she backs up to the street. She has to wait there because Rodell is passing by. I wonder what he's up to at this time of day.

I'm strapped for time to finish off what I intended to do today, but at least I can strike one person off my list. I was going to ask Maddie Hicks if she knew why Caroline left and never came back. No need to trouble her about that now.

CHAPTER 22

As I pull up in front of the Underwood place, I wonder how long Clyde Underwood has known about the racetrack being planned for here in Cotton Hill. Something tells me Frances and Clyde didn't plan on making their home here for long. The place is neglected. The front door has weathered badly, and the siding along the south end of the house is chipped. It gives me a pang to see that a little flower garden delineated by a row of stones has been allowed to go to seed, the plants dead and overrun with weeds. And I don't see a sign of chickens, nor do I hear the background of hen chatter.

Frances Underwood comes to the door and gives me a pinched hello, her eyes sharp and curious as to what I'm doing there. "If you've come for eggs, I'm fresh out," she says.

"I thought maybe you'd got rid of the chickens. You must keep them pretty far from the house."

"That's right," she says. Her voice is flat.

I shouldn't have let on that I suspect she has never kept chickens, but I can't stand a cheat. I know damn good and well that what she did to get close to Dora Lee was buy eggs at the store and bring them around and sell them like they were fresh. But it still seems like a big leap from cheating on eggs to putting a knife in Dora Lee.

"Anyway, I'm not here about eggs. I've come to see you and your husband about a business matter."

"Let me see if Clyde has time to talk to you." She closes the door, leaving me standing on the step, hat in hand. She sure picked up some city ways along the line.

In a minute the door opens again and this time Clyde himself appears. He's a large man with a substantial belly and a large head.

"Come on in, I don't know what Frances was thinking, leaving you standing out here in this heat."

He grabs my arm with his big paw and drags me inside. "Frances, would you get us some tea?" he says.

He sits me down in a parlor that's surely unchanged from when his mother-in-law lived here, and I wonder what they did with the furniture they had in San Antonio. What I suspect is that they had to leave town so fast, they left all their goods behind.

"I understand you were a good friend to Dora Lee Parjeter," Underwood says. "I'm hoping you're here to grease the wheel on this deal I'm trying to make on her land with her heirs."

Frances Underwood carries in a plastic tray with three glasses of iced tea and some store cookies. She sits down with us and hands out the tea. Her husband grabs a handful of cookies and shoves one in his mouth.

"I'm not suited to take a position on that matter," I say. "That's a family thing. I'm here on my own behalf. I'm wondering if a certain rumor I've been hearing is true and hoping I might put a dollar or two into the deal if there's any room."

Underwood's jaw goes slack with surprise. He snatches up his glass of tea and takes a gulp. "I'm not sure what rumor you're talking about."

"I think you do. And I think you offered some incentive money to Wayne Jackson if he would persuade Dora Lee's heirs to sell to you."

Underwood wipes his hand across his mouth. A smile stays on his face, but his eyes get hard. "Did Jackson tell you that? I'm sorry if he got the wrong impression."

I translate that to mean I'm right. "Either way, I'm wondering how I can get in on this racetrack deal."

"Well, now, I guess you have heard a thing or two. And it's true, the deal could use a little more capital. Frances, how about getting that proposal we've put together?"

She slips away, and he confides to me that he doesn't know what he'd do without her, because she's the actual brains behind their business dealings.

I can just imagine the two of them moving in to fleece people who are about to lose everything, him with his glad hand and her with her shrewd mouth.

Frances comes back in with a sleek blue folder and opens it out to reveal copies of official looking papers. She sits down and smoothes her dress over her skinny knees. She may be the brains behind their team, but Clyde presents the deal. I'm surprised how far the plans have proceeded, with mock-up drawings of the track, outbuildings, parking lot, concessions stands, and roads. I can almost hear the sound of those cars revving their engines and smell the odor of oil burning hot.

"Mind if I take a look?" I say.

"Help yourself," Underwood says, shoving the packet around so I can read it. "I can see you're a practiced investor. You'll know what you're looking at."

He'd say that if I were the village idiot. But I've looked over a few proposals in my time as a landman, so I can parse it out. I notice some things right off. Besides the fact that this is a copy of a proposal, and not the original, there is not one mention of the company Jenny said was involved, Best Land Use Enterprises. Second, this proposal is specific to the land Underwood is sitting on and to Dora Lee's land. It's hard for me to believe that a big venture capitalist company would focus on one parcel of land. It seems to me the proposal would be more general. They'd be scouting a few areas.

As I'm reading, trying to figure out how to get my hands on this proposal to take to Houston tomorrow, I hear a siren out on the road. Underwood turns his head to look out the window. "Wonder if there's a fire somewhere," Frances says. There's an uneasy feeling in the room, but maybe it's just me, still on edge after the fire at my place.

I may not know all there is to know about looking over proposals, but I do know the one the Underwoods are peddling has been stolen and rigged up to leave Best Land Use Management out of it.

"How can I get me a copy of this, so I can take my time looking it over?"

"It's not possible for me to let it out of my hands," Underwood says, frowning. "We're trying to keep this quiet. I'm doing you a favor by even letting you look at it."

"Who all is in on it?" I say, all innocent as a babe.

"They want to keep their name under the radar," Underwood says.

"I understand. I appreciate that. I'll tell you what, I've seen what I need to see and I'll take a day or two to think about it."

Underwood shakes his head, his mouth clamped together in a show of regret. "I hope you don't hold out too long. This deal is drawing a lot of interest, and the opportunity is knocking loud and clear. You'd be advised to heed the sound at the door."

Out at my truck, I sit for a minute, trying to imagine either Clyde or Frances Underwood slinking behind my house with kerosene cans and rags, and I don't have a bit of trouble picturing it. But the fact is I'm having a crisis of confidence. What do I think I'm up to, trying to track down who killed Dora Lee and set fire to my place? Time was, I was good at being chief of police. But now I don't have the resources of the department behind me, such as they are. If Rodell were up to the job, I would gladly bow out. But that's the sticking point. And that's what brings me to fire up the truck, determined to see through my investigation, for good or ill.

As soon as I enter the road leading up to Dora Lee's place, I know there's trouble. Half a dozen cars are parked every which way, like people couldn't wait to get out of them and couldn't be bothered to park properly. There's a highway patrol car, Rodell's police car, and Woodrow Callum's fire marshal truck, plus two cars I don't recognize. I jolt to a stop behind them and hurry toward the house, wondering if something has happened to Greg.

I round the side of the house just as Rodell comes out of Greg's cabin. Behind him, two of his lieutenants walk on either side of Greg, whose hands are cuffed behind him. His head is hanging forward so he doesn't see me.

"What the hell is going on here?" I say.

"Welcome to the party," Rodell says.

Greg's head jerks up, and his eyes catch mine, pleading. He's got a cut on one side of his face in the center of a bruise that's beginning to swell.

The two highway patrolmen step over to me. "Sir, back off now! This is police business."

"Why are you taking this boy?" I say.

Rodell waves the patrolmen away. His sneer couldn't be more satisfied. "We've got the goods on your little buddy here. Someone identified him as being near your house the evening it was set on fire. I should think you'd be glad we caught him."

"I already knew he was at my house, you fool! He didn't set fire to it!"

Woodrow Callum has been standing off to the side, and now he comes over and lays his hand on my upper arm. "Samuel, step over here for a minute," he says. "If you all would just hold off," he says to Rodell.

Rodell is enjoying this so much that he'll gladly prolong the moment. Callum steers me away from the group. "I'm afraid we've got the boy dead to rights. I found gas cans and rags out in the shed just like the ones used to torch your place."

"You can buy those things anywhere."

Callum is shaking his head. "These rags have got to be twenty years old. There's a whole stack of them out there. You remember one of the rags used to start your fire had a stamp in one corner? These have the same stamp."

I start to protest that anybody could have stolen those rags out of the shed, but pointing that out is going to have to be Jenny's job, if it goes that far. Rodell is not about to be talked out of his prize right now.

"I understand. Callum, I don't believe Greg was the responsible party, but I can see the evidence looks that way."

Greg's face falls when he sees mine, reading my defeat. "Mr. Craddock, tell them I didn't do it."

I step close to him. "You're going to have to go with them. Don't give them any trouble. Jenny will get you out of jail first thing in the morning."

"But I didn't do it! I'd never set fire to those paintings."

"I know that. You don't have to convince me, but there's evidence that points that way."

"Let's get a move on!" Rodell pushes Greg, who stumbles, and I grab him to keep him upright.

"Step away from the prisoner," the highway patrolman says sharply.

I step back, not wanting to make things any harder for Greg.

The group crowds around Greg as if he's a dangerous fugitive. It would be laughable if it weren't so wrong. I follow as closely as I can. Just as they open the door for Greg to get into the car, he yells back over his shoulder, "Don't let anything happen to my paintings."

"Don't worry," I say.

Just before they leave, Rodell tells them to wait. He struts back to me. Standing with his thumbs hooked in his belt, he shoves his face up close to mine. "I believe you'll find that by tomorrow morning, we'll also have a confession to his grandma's murder."

I grab the front of his shirt and pull him in a couple more inches. "I saw the bruise you left on his face. If there's any more of that, you're going to find yourself in a lawsuit that won't quit."

He knocks my hand away. His face is contorted with fury. "You ain't the law anymore, Craddock. Time has passed you by." He turns on his heels and stalks back to his car.

They're gone in a flurry of dust. I walk over and lower myself onto the back steps, as stunned as if it had been me they arrested. But after a few seconds, I go inside to call Jenny. It's after six, but my guess is she's still in her office, and I'm right.

I tell her what happened. "I don't suppose there's any way to get him out of there tonight?"

"No, Rodell timed it just right. There won't be anyone around to process it. But I'll be there first thing in the morning to get him released."

After that, I go out into Greg's place. A chair is overturned, and I set it up right. I notice he's got three paintings stacked on his bed, his choices to take to the gallery in Houston tomorrow. I'll have to call Manning and Best Land Management first thing in the morning to let them know we won't be there.

When I walk in the door to my place, my phone is ringing. It's Jenny telling me she's bringing home some barbecue, and I should come over there and eat with her. I tell her to give me thirty minutes.

I'm purely worn out. Last night still has its hold on me, and the smell is so bad in here that my head is buzzing. I go in and pack a few things to stay out at Dora Lee's. Whoever torched my house is still at large as far as I'm concerned. And if they know Greg isn't home, that place could be at risk, including Greg's paintings.

The company that has my house and art insured has left a message that an inspector will be by Friday afternoon. There's also a call from a reporter, sounding unsure of himself, saying he's heard something about the theft of a valuable painting. He leaves a number to call back. I erase the message.

As I walk out, I take a look around at my bare walls again. Even though it doesn't feel like home without my paintings on the walls, I still wish I could be here tonight. But the smell of smoke has turned into something nasty, like the water and charred bits have combined to produce a substance all its own that puts out a peculiar odor.

Jenny and I arrive at her place at the same time. "My God, you look whipped," she says.

I point to the big white bag she's carrying along with her briefcase. "I hope you brought enough barbecue. I'd hate to have to argue with you over the last rib."

She laughs her big laugh. It's a welcome sound. When we settle in to eat, I bring her up to date, starting with Callum's assessment that the fire at my place was set deliberately. Then I describe the scene I just witnessed, with Greg being arrested.

"You don't think there's a chance he did it?"

"Setting fire to my place and destroying my art?" I shake my head. "I'm thinking that the fire is connected with my poking around in Dora Lee's affairs."

"You think whoever set the fire killed Dora Lee?"

"It's an awful big coincidence for the fire to happen now, when I've been nosing around. Problem is, I'm damned if I can see the connection."

"A warning maybe?"

"It's too big to be just a warning. If you hadn't been there, the whole place would have gone up. No, it looks like somebody needed money so bad that when they found out I had my art collection, they decided to steal the Thiebaud and sell it, not knowing how hard that would be. The fire was to cover up that theft."

She's nodding. "You said the painting is valuable. How would they know that?"

"That's where Alex Eubanks comes in." I tell her about my interview with the art teacher and his subsequent confrontation with Greg. "Greg told him about my art collection. Eubanks would have known the Thiebaud was valuable."

"But he'd also know you couldn't sell a work of art like that. And if he did kill Dora Lee, why wait six months to do it?"

"You're right, it doesn't quite fit. There has to be something I'm not seeing." I tell her about Eubanks's daughter, and Greg's belief that her father knew nothing about their affair. "Could be he knows more than they think, and he's not happy about it. Could be he was trying to frame Greg. At any rate, as soon as this situation with Greg is resolved, I'm going to sic Callum on him."

"You're right. He ought to at least be ruled out as a serious suspect."

"But there's one more possibility." I tell her what I found out from the real estate people in San Antonio.

She wipes her hands, pushes her plate away, and brings her glass of wine closer. "They could have done both crimes. What do you think?"

"I like them for the fire and theft. But for the murder? What's their motive? If they had come up with a decent price, Dora Lee would have sold. They still would have made a lot of money if the Houston outfit follows through."

"Samuel, we talked about this the other night. Dora Lee might have said she wouldn't sell at any price."

"But they'd have been a lot better off trying to persuade her to sell than waiting for the probate to be done. That could take a year. By then everyone would know the racetrack was going to come in, and that the land was worth a lot of money."

Jenny is shaking her head. "Maybe Dora Lee's murder and the fire at your place aren't connected. So what's your plan?"

I tell her that before Greg was arrested I was going to Houston tomorrow to talk to the racetrack firm. "And then I was planning on taking Greg to meet a gallery owner in Houston."

"You think he's that good?"

"I do. But I want to get a solid opinion to find out if I'm right."

"If I were you, I'd go ahead and keep your appointments in Houston. It could take me half the morning to get Greg out of jail. And you'd just be hanging around being nervous and making everybody crazy. Besides, you'd probably get into it with Rodell, and you don't need that."

CHAPTER 23

I'm awake by five o'clock. If I weren't in a strange bed, I could almost convince myself that the past few days were a dream. I have a sense of dread that I'm never going to figure out who killed Dora Lee and that I'm not going to find my painting or who set the fire at my house. And if that happens, I'm worried that suspicion will always hang over Greg.

Part of being so busy yesterday had the effect of smoothing over events I'd as soon forget, and in the early morning light I bounce my brooding between the loss of the painting Jeanne liked so much and the terrible story Caroline told me. I believe if I'd known what Teague was up to, I would have killed him, or at least called him out to account for his behavior. But I guess a lot of men think they would have been heroes when they look back on events that can't be changed.

Thinking about Caroline, something is nagging at me. Something she said didn't quite fit, but I can't think now what it was.

As soon as the light turns gray, I slip out of bed. I drive to my house and spend some time with my cows, checking them for signs of stress that they get sometimes in the heat. It's a ritual this morning, an exercise I'm doing to bring myself back into a better state. Back at the house, Zelda helps by making sure I keep my mind on her proper care and feeding. She threads herself in and out between my legs, demanding to be petted. I like cats. They are careful to keep their priorities straight. Feed me, give me a warm, dry place to sleep, pet me when I tell you to, then leave me to my own devices.

At seven o'clock I'm back at Dora Lee's farm, drinking coffee and brooding. The more I think about it, the less I like the idea of going over to Houston. I'd like to have Greg with me when I go to Manning's

191

gallery. Finally I convince myself that in spite of what Jenny advised, I'll put off going over there until tomorrow.

I realize that although I've got the address and directions to the Houston outfit I was going to visit today, I don't have their phone number. I'd as soon not have to backtrack to my place before I head to the jail in Bobtail, but I'll have to if I'm going to call. Then I remember I can look it up on the computer.

Dora Lee's computer is still shoved back into a corner of the desk, now with a layer of dust on it. I open it up and wait for the screen to come up. And when it does, I sit staring at it, hardly able to believe what I'm seeing. On the screen is a photo of a landscape oil painting that immediately brings to mind the one missing from over Dora Lee's desk. It's not the same, but close enough so I'm sure it's by the same artist. The artist is William Kern, the man whose obituary Dora Lee had stashed in her mementos.

I scroll down and read the commentary, from an article in the Houston Post a year ago, about the recent resurgence of interest in William Kern's art. Apparently it's considered a perfect example of a pre–World War II style particular to the southwest. Who would have guessed? Then I read on. And eventually I get to the part that says his paintings are now worth around $250,000.

Probably my synapses have slowed at my age, but it still only takes me a few seconds to understand what this means. And to think how much trouble would have been saved if I hadn't assumed Dora Lee wouldn't be much of a computer user. The key to her death has been right here all along.

Wayne Jackson has made a complete mess of my neat piles, shoving Dora Lee's papers into drawers at random. All the business cards are piled haphazardly into one drawer, and it takes me a few minutes to find the one I'm looking for. I tuck it into my shirt pocket.

Now that the trip to Houston is back on, I go out to Greg's cabin, to add a few more paintings to the three he picked out. I look through and bring out one I particularly like, with sunset colors that practically glow off the canvas. It reminds me of the way Rothko's paintings looked in the early days, before they started to fade. And I choose two others, in brooding storm colors. I can't decide which one to take, so I put both of them into Dora Lee's car. I'm driving it so I can transport the paintings in air-conditioning.

Before I leave, I phone Woodrow Callum's office and leave a message telling him he should take a look at Alex Eubanks's alibi for the night the fire was set at my place. I tell him the man had easy access to the gear used to set the fire, and he might have been trying to frame Greg.

Best Land Use Management is in a shiny, slick building in the heart of the city. It has a parking garage underground that will charge me half a week's worth of groceries if I stay there all day. The building is quiet as a church, all chrome and glass and marble. In the lobby a guard keeps out the riff-raff. I tell him I'm here to talk to somebody at Best Land Use about an investment. He looks me up and down and decides I'm not likely to cause too much havoc. He calls up somebody on the phone, and then tells me they'll be expecting me on the eleventh floor.

The elevator is as big as my bathroom at home. I get in and punch the button, take my hat off and smooth my hair back, using the mirror that's all the way around, glad I'm by myself on the elevator with nobody to see me spruce up.

When I get off, I find myself on a floor that is dedicated to this one business. It's all plush carpet and heavy furniture and big potted plants. Their first line of defense is a giant desk, manned by a girl who could be Miss America for all her gleaming smile and abundant hair.

"I don't know exactly who I can talk to, but I believe someone will want to know what I have to tell them." And even as I say it, I figure this little racetrack deal, which seems so big when I'm home in Jarrett County, is probably just a drop in their big bucket.

"What would this be regarding?" She's not unkind, nor in a hurry, just impersonal.

"It's come to my attention that somebody is trying to steal action out from under this outfit," I say.

She frowns. I know this, because two tiny little lines appear between her eyebrows. Otherwise, her facial expression remains smooth. "Let me have you talk to Mr. Lindeman."

I tell her that will be fine, not knowing any better one way or another. At least it's a foot in the door.

Lindeman turns out to be about two years older than Greg, but with years more self-assurance. He takes me to an office that is an inside cubicle, with no view of the city, so I know he isn't high up on the food chain here. I tell him how I came to know about the racetrack they are pondering. When I come to the part about seeing the copied proposal that has been cleaned of their name, he takes a lot more notice.

"Hold on just a minute. I'll be right back." He charges out of there like he's got a burr under his tail.

Before long he's back with a man who introduces himself as Fred Bachman, "please call me Fred." He thanks the young man and before I know it I'm in a handsome office looking out over greater Houston.

Fred is dressed a lot like me, in black denim pants, cowboy boots, and a short-sleeved shirt with a string tie, which puts me at my ease. He doesn't go behind his desk, but sits down in an easy chair facing me. I repeat my story while Fred sits reared back with his hands laced behind his head, and one leg crossed over at the knee. He nods from time to time.

"The racetrack is one of our interests," he says. "We've got a few feelers out about where to build it. I know the area you're talking about in Cotton Hill. I don't know what it will come to, but it's one of several sites we're considering."

"That's what I figured."

"Now what I want to know is why you've taken the trouble to bring these people to my attention?"

"You mean do I want something out of tattling to you about the Underwoods?"

He nods.

"Nothing financial, if that's what you're thinking. Clyde Underwood doesn't sit well with me. He has the ability to cause some problems for a young man of my acquaintance whose grandma just passed away. All I want is to see to it that the boy isn't swindled out of his share of her land."

He looks at me long and hard. "Are you looking to invest with us?" he says.

I laugh. "No sir, I've got my own interests, and I wouldn't know the first thing about a racetrack."

He nods. "And you wouldn't care to have one in your area, I suppose. The noise, the influx of outside people . . ."

I see where he's headed. He wants to know if my fuss about the Underwoods is just an excuse to get the company to look somewhere else to put their racetrack. "Well, sir, that doesn't concern me so much. That's for the people who live close by to decide, whether the prosperity it would bring would offset the negatives. As it happens I don't live near there, so the only part of this that's my business is like I said, the boy's being properly taken care of."

He tips forward and leans toward me. "Let me assure you of two things. If we do decide that this area is where we want to proceed, we'll be offering better than fair money for the land."

"And the Underwoods?" I say.

"I'm going to level with you," he says. "Mr. and Mrs. Underwood are known to our company. They have indicated that they were interested in being a part of this investment. Now it seems they've decided to grab a bigger chunk. We don't look kindly on that. I suspect before too long that the Underwoods will find it in their best interest to move on. They may even be wanting to sell their land to anyone who might be interested." He raises his eyebrows to indicate that I might just be that person.

"Don't look at me. I want no part of it. But I appreciate your taking it seriously, and I'll leave you to your business."

"All right, then. I guess all I can do for you is to shake your hand and thank you." He blinks. "There is something. You interested in baseball?"

I smile. "I enjoy a game." I'm really not much interested in baseball outside our little league in Jarrett Creek, but I can see he wants to do something to pay me back for my information. It will leave him feeling like he doesn't owe me. And I know someone else who likes baseball.

He goes out for a time and comes back with an envelope. "See if you can use these," he says. I look at the two tickets, which are for an Astros game a couple of weeks from now. I give him a big grin, as if I know where the seats are, to let him know how pleased I am.

"And I'd like to put you up at the Four Seasons that night, so you don't have to drive right back home afterwards. Just ask for the room in your name, and it will be ready for you."

"That's very kind. I'll take you up on it. Sounds like a good time."

He sees me to the front desk and has the receptionist stamp my parking ticket. It seems that with the magic stamp I won't have to pay a dime. We part with hearty handshakes and good will all around. Once I'm outside, I allow myself to feel the satisfaction of knowing the Underwoods are going to reap what they've sowed. But I don't get to stick with the feeling long. I still don't know if they had anything to do with Dora Lee's death or the theft of my art, and at the moment I don't feel any closer to knowing who did either crime.

CHAPTER 24

I t's only eleven o'clock, so I stop at a little café near the art gallery for an early lunch. Jeanne and I ate there a time or two and they have substantial sandwiches. While I eat, I let memories of Jeanne's and my excursions to the gallery drift through my mind. I would love to have shared with her my excitement about Greg's paintings. Suddenly I have a sinking of the heart, hoping I haven't raised Greg's expectations for nothing. Manning will be polite, I know that. Even if he doesn't see much promise in the pieces I've brought, he'll say that Greg should keep at his work, and to come back in a few years, when he has matured. He'll tell me Greg needs to go to art school. But I'm hoping for more than that, and I know Greg is, too. I'm sure Manning won't be calling a press conference, saying he has the next de Kooning or Rauschenberg on his hands, but somewhere in between would be nice.

Before I leave the café, I use their pay phone to call Jenny to find out if Greg has been released. But I just get her answering machine.

When I walk into Manning's gallery, the woman who relieves me of Greg's canvasses tells me that Mr. Manning will be in soon. In fact I'm half an hour early, so I use the time to look at the works he has up for sale. Manning has all kinds of art. Every dealer has to have variety. But it's clear his taste tends toward the contemporary.

I stop in front of a small painting that takes my eye by a woman I've never heard of, Melinda Buie, and all at once I miss Jeanne so much I almost have to walk outside to gather myself. Her presence is strong with me most of the time, but this is a different order altogether. I can hear her lilting voice exclaiming over the virtues of the painting, see her eyes alight with the pleasure of sharing an artist's passion.

All of a sudden Manning is at my elbow. "This reminds me of a couple of the pictures you and Jeanne bought," he says. "You ought to think about buying it."

My voice is a croak. "I haven't thought about adding to my collection for a while now."

"It would fit right in," he says, not knowing what a gift he has given me. I can still have Jeanne with me if I am willing to make a bold purchase on my own.

"I'll sure think about it."

Manning glances around the room, which is empty except for me. "I thought the artist was coming with you."

I tell him that something came up, and that rather than reschedule, I decided to keep our appointment. "I can bring him back another time," I say.

"Fine. Maybe that's best anyway, to let me make an assessment before I meet him. Let's take a look at what you've brought."

The woman who greeted me when I first came in has taken Greg's pieces to a back room and set them up on easels in their own little show. Seeing them set up like this, I realize that I was anxious that they would diminish in this world of proven art. But I needn't have worried. As the woman who set them up leaves the room, I see in her eyes that I've not been mistaken. She casts a glance at me that combines the calculation of a dealer with the wonder of discovery.

Manning takes his time, pausing in front of each one to take in the whole of it. The longer he takes, the more I relax. I've heard the art world described as being as fickle and unkind and capricious as a jaded coquette. Sometimes she makes mistakes and takes a temporary lover who in the end doesn't suit. But she recognizes the best when she sees it, and embraces it. Finally Manning begins to nod.

He turns. "How long has this artist been painting?" he asks.

"Since he was kid," I say. And then I laugh. "He's only twenty-two."

"Twenty-two?" Manning shakes his head.

"His daddy painted some, and I guess Greg took to it right away."

Manning puts his hand to his chin and strokes it, his eyes inward. "What was his father's name?"

"Oliver Marcus. But you wouldn't have heard of him. He and Greg are light years apart."

"Well, he certainly passed something onto Greg. Now let me think what I can do with this work. I'll be right back."

I'm wishing like hell that Greg could be here with me to watch Manning take his painting seriously. But I have a feeling he's going to see the reaction many times in his life.

While I wait for Manning to return, my eye is drawn to a bunch of landscapes standing in a row on the floor against the wall. They must have been on these easels, and taken down to display Greg's paintings. I suppose Manning keeps them in this back room because it isn't really his style. I normally wouldn't give them a moment's notice, but one of them in particular catches my interest.

Manning returns, rubbing his hands like someone about to throw the dice. "If it's all right, I'd like to keep these pictures. I want to show them to a couple of people. It's a hard time in the art world right now, but I know some people who like to encourage young artists."

I tell him I'm sure Greg will be happy for me to leave them. Then I point to the landscape that caught my attention. "George, is that by William Kern?"

Manning glances at the landscapes propped against the wall. "Yes, it is. Good call. I wouldn't have thought he'd interest you, but he's very popular right now." He takes one of Greg's pictures off its easel and leans it against the wall and puts the small landscape in its place.

"Kern was never appreciated in his lifetime, but it's one of those art things that drives a dealer crazy. He's come into fashion, and his work is selling like hotcakes. Unfortunately this one is sold, but I can try to find you one if you like it." He steps back and looks at it critically. "As you know, this kind of art really isn't in my line, I just happened to come by this one a few years ago when I bought an estate collection. And I'm certainly glad I did. This sale is going to keep my gallery going for some time. How did you recognize it?"

"I know someone who has one."

"You tell whoever owns it that if they have a mind to sell it, there will never be a better time."

And just like that my memory clicks into place. I can see Caroline standing with the article about William Kern in her hand, telling me I can throw it away because her mother sold the piece a while back. Wayne said so. And my question is, if Wayne hadn't seen Dora Lee since he was a boy, how did he know that?

"Do you know a gallery called Houston Antiques 'N Art?" I ask Manning.

He takes a second to respond. "It's not really a gallery. More like an antique store, loosely speaking. I don't know it well, but I've met the owner, Dallas Morton. He's got a good reputation. Why do you ask?"

"I wonder if you would mind calling him for me and giving me an introduction. I need to go and see him while I'm in town."

He says he'll be glad to do that. While he phones Morton, I try Jenny again. This time she answers, but her voice is so quiet I can barely hear her. "Samuel," she whispers, "Greg's back home. I'm in court. Can't talk." She switches off. But I've heard all I need to.

When Manning returns, he escorts me to the door. I pause to take one more look at the Buie painting and tell Manning that if he wouldn't mind, I'd like him to set it aside for a few days, that I'd like to mull over the purchase of it.

"Take your time," he says. "And with the market being what it is, I think I can get you a good price for it."

CHAPTER 25

Even with Manning's precise directions, I get good and lost. Houston is a sprawling city that covers a lot of territory, with freeways that are so badly marked that you'd think the city planners' philosophy is that if you don't know where you're going, you shouldn't be here. My frustration is compounded by the turmoil in my head. I'd been ready to believe that the owner, Dallas Morton, was a killer who had taken advantage of an old woman's vulnerability. But now my thoughts are tending another way. I'm impatient to get to the heart of the matter.

Finally I find Houston Antiques 'N Art, located in a mall that stretches about as big as Dora Lee's farm. The place is completely different from Manning's gallery. It looks like a warehouse, crammed up tight with fine pieces of furniture butted up next to some of the ugliest junk I've ever laid eyes on.

When Dallas Morton greets me, I recognize his voice from when I called Houston Antiques 'N Art right after Dora Lee was killed, trying to find out if Caroline might work there. It seems like an age ago. But now at least I have an inkling of why this man's card was in Dora Lee's possession.

Morton is a rangy man who wears clothes that makes him look like he's ready to grab his partner at a square dance. His pale blue shirt has ruffles down the front and he's wearing tight black pants and cowboy boots with high heels. It's all finished off with a bolo tie with a piece of turquoise the size of my fist. He wears a silver and turquoise bracelet and rings to match.

I introduce myself, and Morton tells me he's pleased to help me any way he can. I expect by the time we're done he'll change his mind about that. He takes me into his office so we can speak privately. Even Morton's office has its share of goods, stacked in corners and around on the floor.

"Excuse the mess," he says. "We're finding these days that people are in need of money, and we're getting more consignments than we usually do. I'm going to have to rent some warehouse space. I may be one of the few businessmen in town looking to hire someone to help me, rather than laying off."

He sits us down in chairs constructed of elk horn that are more comfortable than they look.

"So you're selling as well as buying," I say. It pays to ease into difficult subjects with a little small talk.

He touches the turquoise holding his tie, like it's a talisman. "Yes, I'm probably the biggest purveyor of antique goods in Texas, and people from all over contact me when they're in need of a particular piece."

"You buy and sell art as well as antiques?"

"That's actually how I started out. If I could wave a magic wand right now, I'd have the kind of storefront that George Manning runs. But it didn't work out that way. One thing led to another, and this is the result." He gestures in the direction of his showroom. "Now, George said you had something particular you needed. What can I do for you?"

"Let me start back a week or so ago," I say. "I called here and I think I talked to you, asking if you'd ever had someone stop in by the name of Parjeter."

He nods. "I do remember that. You were trying to find someone you thought might have worked here. Did you ever find who you were looking for?"

"Thank you, I did. But I'm afraid that wasn't the end of it. Let me ask you, just to be clear. You ever meet a woman by the name of Dora Lee Parjeter?"

"Like I told you at the time. Never heard of her, never even heard the name."

I take a deep breath. Either he's lying, or something else is in play.

"Then I need to ask you if you've ever had dealings with a man by the name of Wayne Jackson."

He hesitates, then nods. "Yes, I have."

"He brought a picture in here painted by William Kern?"

"That would be correct."

"How did he say he came to be in possession of the picture?"

He hesitates a little longer this time. "He told me he was representing his aunt. He said she was shy of coming in herself and that he was helping her out."

"He never mentioned his aunt's name?"

Morton grimaces. "No. I pressed him on it, but he said she preferred to be kept out of it."

"Have you sold the painting?"

"I have an interested buyer." He's been shifting around in his seat. "I'm sorry, but I need to find out why you're asking me these questions. George Manning vouched for you, but it would help me out if you could tell me what this is about."

Now it's my turn to squirm. I don't want to tell him just yet that Dora Lee was killed. I need to know for sure that I'm on the right track. "Dora Lee Parjeter is Jackson's aunt. She's an old friend of mine. I expect she asked for her nephew's help because she didn't want to be hoodwinked. She has lived most of her life in the country, and she's worried about city folks."

He's nodding. "We get that with a lot of these old people. Even someone who has lived here in Houston his whole life can worry that they are going to lose what little they've got and be penniless in the end. I won't say I'm not close with a dollar, but I'm not a cheat, and I try to do right by my customers."

I put up my hand. "There's no question of your integrity. The question is Jackson's integrity. George Manning told me what these paintings can go for. We're talking in the vicinity of a quarter million dollars for this picture?"

"Possibly more. But we're proceeding cautiously. The buyer I've shown it to wants to know the provenance, which I understand. Mr. Jackson had told me that the picture was in the family's possession ever since it was painted, and I asked him to get some sworn statements to that effect."

"When did you ask him this?"

"A few days ago."

I sigh, feeling the relief of having the connection finally fall into place. Jackson thought he was going to get the money from the sale of Dora Lee's painting without anybody ever knowing about it. But when he was asked to prove ownership, he saw that money slip away. He couldn't let on to anyone that he had the painting without being suspected of her murder. He must have had all kinds of plans for that money. And that's where my Thiebaud came in. Finding out I had art worth stealing must have seemed like a reprieve. And who would ever suspect him of either crime?

Morton is watching me. He's turning one of his big silver and turquoise rings around and around on his finger. "Is there a problem with Jackson?"

"I'm afraid so."

"You mean he won't be able to establish ownership?"

"Oh, I can tell you Dora Lee owned the painting. I've known her since it was bought."

"That's good to know. Can you tell me anything about the circumstances of when it was bought?"

"Dora Lee's family moved to Austin for a year or two when she was a teenaged girl, and her mother bought it. I don't exactly know why. They aren't really a type of family that would have been looking to buy art."

He laughs. "At that time it wouldn't have been considered what we call 'art.' Somebody would have seen it and said, 'oh that's a pretty picture.' They probably only paid a few dollars for it."

"Do you mind if I take a look at it, make sure we're talking about the same piece?"

"It's in a vault, but I've got some good photos of it."

He opens the lid on a white computer on his desk and begins to punch in information. After a minute, he turns it around so I can see it.

"That's it. It's funny, when I saw it was missing off the wall, I couldn't recall it. It's one of those things you see and don't see."

Morton clears his throat. "What I'm concerned about is if there's a problem with Jackson selling it. He signed an agreement with me and there would be a small penalty involved if the family wants it back. I'd hate to see this become a legal issue."

"I don't think the family will mind selling the picture, though I'll have to verify that with the rightful heirs. But I do have one more question. When Mr. Jackson came in here, did he have any idea what this picture was worth?"

Morton claps his hands together and laughs. "Oh, not at all. When he walked in here, he was in a hurry, impatient to get his mission over with. He said he'd agreed to bring this to me to help his aunt because she seemed to think it was worth something. It took me some time to make sure I knew what I was looking at. I took it out of the cheap little frame it was in and found the signature, half-covered up. Luckily the painting doesn't ever seem to have been damaged by light. I told him I had to verify it with people who knew more about it than I did, but I figured it might fetch as much as three hundred and fifty thousand dollars." He laughs again. "You could have knocked him over with a feather."

I can see how it would have worked out. Jackson thought when he walked in here that he was going to be able to get Dora Lee at most a few hundred dollars. I can't even imagine what his thought process must have been when he found out she was right after all, and it was truly valuable.

"I guess I ought to tell you what my thinking is," I say, "so you'll be prepared."

Dallas Morton puts his hand to the lump of turquoise on his tie again. "Go ahead."

"The owner of that picture, Dora Lee Parjeter, was murdered a week ago. They buried her Monday."

He claps his hand to his heart. "Oh, my heavens, I'm so sorry to hear that. That's a terrible thing to happen to an old woman." He pauses and I can see he's working something out that troubles him. "Do they know who did it?"

"They haven't figured that out yet, but I'm thinking it won't be long now."

"You're thinking this painting might have something to do with it," he says, his tone matter of fact.

"I don't want to jump to false conclusions, but it's tending that way."

He hunches himself forward over his desk. "I should tell you that when I told Mr. Jackson he'd need to verify the painting's history, he got pretty agitated. He seemed to want the deal to be over with in a hurry. I've been in this business thirty plus years, and somebody wanting to rush things is never a good sign."

"I can see how that would be the case."

"It wouldn't be the first time some relative tried to pull a fast one on the other members of his family. I told Mr. Jackson that this was a slow-moving business, and we had no need to rush."

I sigh, thinking that if Morton had told Jackson that he needed verification of the painting's ownership the first time he came in, Dora Lee might be alive today.

"There's one other thing. It's not pretty, but it's true. If this painting is associated with the owner's death, it's only going to increase in value. Some of these buyers of historical artists relish the thought of having it associated with a little violence."

"That would be interesting information, if the violence didn't concern the murder of a friend of mine." I can't help the sharp tone of my voice. I think of Dora Lee lying on that kitchen floor, and my share in leaving her unprotected.

"An unsavory part of the antique business."

I get up. "I'd appreciate it if you'd give me a couple of days to sort out the family interest."

Morton says he'll be waiting for my call.

I'd give anything if I could head on home and wait for the painting to sell and forget the bad things associated with it. But the bad part is just getting started. I don't know exactly how I'm going to proceed with Jackson. If he actually did what I think he did, he's a dangerous man, and I'm not a lawman myself, not anymore. But who do I pull into it? Do I go to the Houston police and talk it over with them? The very idea makes me sweat.

But there's surely no percentage in telling Rodell. He'd have no interest in proving me right. What comes to mind is that I'll talk to the fire marshal in Bobtail and find out who he thinks is a person on the Bobtail police force worth bringing my information to. But that means I have to be damn sure of the facts.

This is one time I wish I had me a cell phone, even if it doesn't work out in Jarrett Creek. I find a service station and use their phone to call Jenny and tell her what I need.

"You don't ask for much, do you?" she says. "I'll get on my computer and be back with you in a few minutes."

It's more like twenty minutes, and I'm about to die standing out in the heat. Even though it's getting to be late afternoon, the sun is still going strong. And the humidity makes it worse. Towering, dark clouds are forming up out east, over the gulf, and I imagine it will rain before the night is over.

When Jenny gets back to me, she apologizes for taking so long. "But I have actual work to do as well as fetch and carry for you." Using a lot more computer savvy than I have, she has pinned down the name and address of Wayne Jackson's business, which turns out to be an electronics store. When I tell her I wonder how I'd get there from here, she says, "If you'll tell me where you are, I'll get directions."

Before long she's telling me what I need to know. I jot down the basics on the back of the card Morton gave me on my way out of his place. And then I rush back to the car. It's almost five o'clock, and I want to get there before they close for the day. I want to see what I can find out about the financial situation of Jackson's business from whoever he has working there. They won't know the whole of it, I imagine, and I may have a hard time getting them to tell me much, but they can at least tell me whether business has fallen off. It occurs to me that I might even find Jackson there, but I'll have to take care of that bridge when it looms up.

CHAPTER 26

The *Going out of Business* signs plastered all over W. L. Electronics's windows tell me I'm headed down the right trail. I go inside, trying to decide how I'm going to approach Jackson if he's there.

If W. L. Electronics were my business, I would feel bad seeing the dwindling stock and taking note of the general gloom. The heavy girl with tattoos and a pierced nose who comes over to ask me if she can help me has a listless attitude. "Is the owner here?" I say.

"No, but his wife is in the back going over the books. Ex-wife. Whatever."

"I'd like to speak with her." I have not one clue what I'll say to her, but I'll think of something.

The tattooed girl hauls herself off and returns in a minute with a pretty woman chasing fifty, dressed in jeans and a faded T-shirt. Her gray-streaked hair is pulled back in a ponytail, which gives her a youthful look at odds with her haunted eyes. She tells me her name is Anne Jackson.

"Ma'am, I'm Samuel Craddock. I was a friend of your husband's aunt Dora Lee who died last week."

She puts a hand up to her throat. "That was sad. Wayne was so upset. He said he felt like he was trespassing going out to her farm, but that he just had to do something."

He did something all right. I wonder if she has the faintest idea that her ex-husband probably killed Dora Lee. I survey the store. "Looks like you all have been a victim of the economy."

She follows my gaze. I'm sure she sees the depleted shelves in her sleep. "I don't know what we're going to do. We built this business together, and even when a Best Buy went in a few blocks over, we managed to do okay. But money got tight . . . well, you don't need to hear my problems."

"I don't mind listening. Sometimes it helps to lay things out, even to a stranger." A stranger who's a snake in the grass.

She smiles, and I wonder what drove her and her husband apart. I've seen a shortage of money make people bitter, and they turn on each other out of frustration.

"The hardest part for Wayne is that he's going to have to go to his step-father and tell him he's lost the business."

"I guess the *L* in W. L. Electronics stands for Leslie?"

"You know Leslie?"

"Met him after Dora Lee died."

"He loaned us money to get the business off the ground, and he never let Wayne forget it for a minute."

I think about how hard it would be to go hat in hand to that miserly old man and tell him you'd lost his money. "Wayne didn't tell him the business was in trouble?"

"He kept hoping there would be a miracle."

"You have kids?" I say.

"Two sons and a daughter. Our oldest boy, Todd, is about to go off to college." Her voice trails away. She doesn't need to tell me that with their financial situation, that's not likely to happen.

My heart sinks further at the idea that those three kids are going to have to live with what their daddy has done. Maybe I'm wrong, maybe it's a coincidence that Dora Lee asked Wayne to help her sell a valuable painting, and then she showed up dead. But if it's a coincidence, how come he hasn't mentioned the painting to anyone? And how come he told Caroline that Dora Lee had sold the painting long ago?

"Can you tell me where your husband is? I'd like to have a word with him."

She studies my face. I hope it doesn't give anything away. She'll know what he's done soon enough. "Laurel said he came by this morning and then said he had some errands to run."

"Do you have a phone number where I might reach him? I just have a couple things I'd like to go over with him about dispensing with Dora Lee's estate."

"Oh, I see. Let me call him at his apartment. He was thinking about having the phone cut off to save money, but I don't know if he's done it yet. Come on back with me, and you can talk to him."

I follow her to a tiny little back office, where she has been working. There are papers spread out on the metal desk with figures on them and penciled notations. "You keep the books?" I say.

"No, Wayne did that. But I decided I should go over them, too, so I'd know exactly what we're up against. I sometimes think if I had taken an interest sooner, I could have pulled us out. He was so distracted."

She sits behind the desk and dials a number. She listens and shakes her head. "It's cut off. Let me try his cell phone." She dials again and leaves a message for him to get back to her. She sits very still for a minute, thunder gathering in her face. "There's one other number I could try, I guess. He said it was only for emergencies with the kids."

The fury in her eyes and the extra phone number lay it all out for me. Wayne most likely spent money he didn't have to make some other woman happy.

Her phone rings and when she answers it, her face hardens. "There's a Mr. Craddock here to see you." She pauses. "Well, what should I tell him?" She looks startled and then hangs up the phone. Her cheeks are flushed.

"He's not in a good state of mind. But there's no need to be rude."

"I'm wondering if you would mind giving me his address, so I can stop by and see him."

"He's not home. He said he's on his way back out to Dora Lee's. He says he has a couple of things he left undone."

Something about that turn of phrase troubles me. But at least I know I'm through here. I thank her and start to leave, but then I think of one more thing. "Could you tell me what kind of car you drive?"

"A BMW. Why?"

"Did you ever lend it to your husband?"

"Lend it? No. He had it for a few days a couple of weeks ago. He wanted to take it to a dealer to see what he could get for it. He said the payments are too high and we'll have to sell it."

"A convertible?" I say.

"Yes, how did you know?"

"Just a guess."

As I head for my car, the first fat drops of rain spatter on the sidewalk.

CHAPTER 27

The further I drive toward home, the more anxious I get. What could Wayne have meant that he left something undone? And then, all of a sudden I know what he's planning just as sure as if he'd told me. Which in a way, he has. And as if to make matters worse, the clouds I saw earlier have caught up with me and rain is starting to come down in great slashes.

In spite of the hard rain, I speed up. While I rocket along, windshield wipers barely keeping up with the downpour, I get more and more agitated. I have no idea when Jackson left. He can't be in Cotton Hill yet, because his cell phone worked when his ex-wife called him, but he could be too far along for me to catch up to him. And the more I think about it, the more I think I'd better stop and make a call to Elvin Crown.

I'm on a freeway northwest of Houston and I look for an exit that has a sign saying there are gas stations. But this is an industrial part of town and I pass two exits, and drive another ten minutes before I see a place that likely has a telephone. If I know Dora Lee at all, she keeps an umbrella in the car. Sure enough, there's one on the floor in the back seat, and I'm glad for it, because the telephone is on the outside of the service station.

Not knowing Elvin's phone number right off, I have to call the information operator, and she tells me there is no such person. "But I know the man, and I know he has a phone."

"Maybe his number is unlisted." If she was any more disinterested, she'd be comatose.

There's no use arguing with her, so I hang up and call Loretta. I don't want to, but I know she'll help me out.

As soon as she hears my voice, Loretta starts in about the headstones she and Ida Ruth saw today.

"Loretta, we can talk about that later. I'm in a fix now and need your help."

"What kind of a fix? And what's that noise? Where are you?"

"I'm in Houston and it's pouring rain. I'll tell you everything later, but now I need your help. Listen to me. Call Elvin and get his volunteer firemen out to Dora Lee's."

"Oh, my Lord. Is there a fire?"

"Not yet, but I believe there will be soon."

"Samuel, that doesn't make any sense," she says.

"Tell Elvin I'll explain it to him when I get there. I'm about an hour out from Cotton Hill."

I finally convince her to call him. Back on the road, I don't slow down, but at least I feel better about the chances.

The drive to Cotton Hill seems like it takes about ten hours. I'm grateful when I finally outrun the storm.

It's getting on for dusk by the time I pull off the road and head for the farm. I peer at the skies but don't see any sign of smoke or light.

I'm surprised not to see more cars at Dora Lee's. There's my pickup and Elvin's car, and Jackson's SUV. The house is dark except for a light in the kitchen. I'm trying to work out how I'm going to approach this.

I get out of the car and jigger my leg back and forth to get the kinks out of my knee. I go over to my pickup and take my cane out of the back. It's a decent weapon, not one of those aluminum jobs, but a substantial oak stick that Truly Bennett carved for me. When I mount the kitchen steps, I don't hear anyone talking. I wonder where Elvin is. I try to open the door, but it's locked. Someone is moving around inside. I rap hard on the door and the movement stops. "Jackson, I need to talk to you," I call out. "It'll only take a minute."

Saying those words take me back into my days as a lawman. They are words that never bode well for whoever is on the other side of the door.

His steps come close to the door. "I can't talk to you right now. You go on home."

"Open the door, Wayne. I can make things a good sight easier for you, if we sit down and talk."

Suddenly the door opens. Jackson looms up, and I get a whiff of menace that raises my neck hair.

"I don't know what you want," he says. "But I don't have time to sit down for a little chat with you. I'm busy."

"So busy you can't indulge your aunt's old friend?"

"I have to get on back to Houston tonight. I just came to pick up a few things I left." He mops his face with his handkerchief.

"That's Elvin Crown's pickup out there. Is he inside with you?"

"I just got here. I have no idea about any Elvin."

"I need to talk to you about that deal you have with the Underwoods."

He hesitates. This is the least of his crimes. I know he's thinking that I'm a fool, and that if he can talk his way out of his part in that deal, he can head back to Houston and get away with everything else. "All right, come on in here." And he does a curious thing. He glances back behind him to the part of the house beyond the kitchen. "But make it quick."

I take my time, being an old man with a bum leg and probably a little demented besides. I tell him I'm awfully thirsty and get myself a drink of water and make my way slowly over to sit down at the kitchen table. Wayne doesn't sit until I tell him to in as friendly a way as I can muster. I'm pretty sure he doesn't know he's got a smear of blood on his pants. That gives me a bad feeling about Elvin. I wonder if Wayne thinks I can't smell the kerosene on him. I wonder where he has stashed the cans he planned to light this place up with.

"I think I ought to give you some friendly advice," I say.

"I can't think what kind of advice I'd need from you."

"Oh, you might find this interesting. In the next few days, Frances and Clyde Underwood are going to clear out of here. Their scheme to grab up the land that's under consideration for a racetrack has been found out, and your part of it no longer applies."

His eyes squint up. "I don't have anything to do with the Underwoods."

"Oh, I wish you wouldn't try to weasel out on this. I know they were going to cut you in on their deal if you could get Caroline and Greg to sell them their land. They planned to make a pack of money on it."

"If you say so," he says.

"I do. And what I need to tell you is that the big outfit in Houston that actually put the deal together didn't take kindly to someone stealing their plans."

He nods and trots out a phony smile. "I'm still not saying I had anything to do with the Underwoods, but I appreciate your letting me know about this. If that's all, then I need to be on my way."

Jackson has perked up now that his desperate plans don't have to be carried out. I figured out that he was going to set fire to the house and cabin. The idea was that if Greg was arrested, and when he got out of jail there was no place for him to come back to, he'd be more willing to sell to the Underwoods. Then Jackson would get the money they'd promised him out of the deal.

"No, Wayne, that's not all. I need to talk to you about my painting."

"Your painting? I don't know what you mean."

"The one you stole from my place and set the fire to cover it up."

He stands up, his eyes dark and angry. "I never did any such thing."

I lay my hands flat on the table, as if gentling down a spooky dog. "The deal I'm willing to make you is this. If you just get it back to me unharmed, I'll forget about the fire and tell the insurance company I was careless with some flammables. They'll believe that as long as they don't have to pay out for that painting. Then you could just go on your way."

"That would sound like a good deal, if I had anything to do with it, but you've got the wrong man."

"Here's the thing you need to know. With a painting that valuable, the insurance company is going to be sending an investigator, and you can be pretty sure they'll pursue every possibility."

His face is all twisted up. "Well, what if they were to think what I think, that you took the painting off somewhere and set fire to your own place for the insurance money?"

Suddenly I hear something from the front of the house that sounds like a groan. Jackson's head snaps up. He looks toward the sound. Being an old man, my hearing can't be all that good, so I pretend I didn't hear a thing.

"The problem you have is that somebody saw you that night. I have an old neighbor who keeps a pretty sharp eye out. She described you pretty well." A lie I don't feel one bit bad about telling.

He's got some panic in his eyes now, and he clenches and unclenches his fists. I calculate my chances if he attacks me. He's bigger than me, no doubt, but he's a city man, soft in the middle. I'm smaller than he is, but wiry, and except for my bum knee, I keep pretty fit. He's got another advantage, fear and anger at being cornered. But I've got my zeal for self-preservation on my side. It has boosted me out of a few tough situations. I believe that we are evenly matched. I stand up.

"You're a criminal. I'm giving you an opportunity to walk away. I met your nice wife this afternoon, and I know you've got kids. They're not going to want to find out their daddy stole a valuable painting."

I have no intention of letting him walk away from killing Dora Lee, of course, but I'd like to get my Thiebaud back before I go on to the next subject. "What do you say?"

No telling what he would have said, because just then the back door opens, and Loretta says, "What in the world is going on out here?"

Just as Jackson turns his head to look at her, I lash out with a punch, landing it square on his jaw. I put everything I've got into it, which isn't as much as it used to be, but is enough to stagger him. To follow up my momentary advantage, I pick up my cane and bring it down hard at the back of his ear. He sags to his knees. It's not like the movies, where people get hit and then come back for more. A good blow usually works long enough to get the situation under control.

Loretta is screaming.

"Loretta, be quiet! Go get Greg. Now!"

She tears out the back door. I whip off my belt and hoist Jackson's hands behind him and tie them up as best I can. It won't stop him long, but long enough for me to find some tape. I rush into the laundry room and grab at boxes until I find duct tape. Back in the kitchen, I run the duct tape around Jackson's legs. He's stirring, but with his legs tied up he can't go anywhere. I do the same with his hands. Just as I'm done, he comes to enough to realize he's trussed up. He starts to bellow.

Loretta and Greg come pounding into the room. I see car beams through the kitchen window and someone drives up. In a half a minute Rodell strolls in through the back door, red eyes blinking at the sight before his eyes.

"What the hell's going on here? Why have you got Jackson all tied up? And where's Elvin?"

"Jackson killed Dora Lee," I say.

"The hell he did!"

I hear groaning from the other room. I'm glad that Elvin isn't dead, and even gladder that he didn't die in the fire Jackson had planned to set.

"Go on in the front room there and help Elvin," I say. "I hear him groaning in there. Jackson must have done something to him. Lucky he didn't kill him. And call your troops to get out here."

Being ordered around seems to suit Rodell, since things seem to be out of his control. He scoots out of the kitchen.

I tell Loretta to stop making a fuss and if she needs something to do, get us some coffee. I send Greg to find some rope so I can secure Jackson a little better. It occurs to me that my success in corralling Jackson has made me a little bossy.

Once Rodell gets going, he doesn't hold back and before long the whole police force of Jarrett County arrives along with the highway patrol and they haul Jackson out of there.

CHAPTER 28

There's hardly anything I like about the next few days. It takes some time to find my Thiebaud, and in the end it's Jackson's poor wife who finds it stashed in his apartment along with about $20,000 in cash that he's systematically skimmed off the business. I meet her at the apartment to pick up the painting.

Anne greets me at the door. Her eyes are sunk so deep in shadows that she looks like somebody gave her two black eyes. She asks me to have a glass of iced tea with her, and I can't turn down the chance to talk to her. I'm still hoping to understand something about Jackson's turn of mind.

"I blame his daddy," Anne says. "He was a miser in every sense of the word. He couldn't spare a drop of affection for Wayne. Poor Wayne did everything to try to get that dried-up old man's approval."

"Wayne managed to marry a fine woman and raise three kids," I say. "I just wonder why that wasn't enough for him."

"I've asked myself that same thing. You heard about the money I found? How could he have kept that from his kids?" She's crying now, which seems to me to be the right response.

"Maybe he thought he could invest it somewhere and surprise you with making a lot more of it. It seems to me when somebody starts out not having enough money and not having approval from their parents, it's hard to catch up. Seems like maybe Wayne was always trying to get over that hump."

She wipes tears from her face. "It's good of you to put it that way. It's something I can tell my kids to help them cope with what he's done."

She tells me they're going to have to move out of Houston. "The kids won't be able to hold their heads up here."

"Where will you go?"

"My folks live down around Corpus Christi. I'd like to be closer to them anyway."

After I leave her, I'm not nearly done with the hard things. My next stop is to meet the curator of the Houston Museum of Modern Art. I turned down his suggestion that he invite the whole board to have a big dinner with me to celebrate my temporary gift of the Thiebaud. So it's just the two of us meeting.

Before I go inside, I take the Thiebaud out of the packing I've wrapped it in and take a good long look at it. Giving it up feels like giving away a little part of Jeanne. This museum will have to turn it over to the Modern Art Museum in Fort Worth when I die, as Jeanne wanted, but I'm giving the Houston museum temporary custody because I want the painting to be close enough so it will be easy to visit.

The curator has still managed to fuss up our meeting with a little bit of pomp. The president of the board and his tiny little wife are there to shake my hand. They've already given me what I wanted in return, and that is a guaranteed place for Greg at the University of Texas in the art school. I'm not pleased with the fact that they did it just on my word and never even asked to see any of Greg's work. It makes me wonder how many places in art schools are taken up by people who get there by money rather than talent. But I can't solve the problems of the world; I can just do what I can for one artist.

My last call has to be in the early evening, because Caroline doesn't get off work until six o'clock. I've arranged to take her out to dinner, telling her I want to discuss financial matters. It took me some time to track her down, since she wouldn't return her phone calls and I had to find her at her place of work.

We go to an Italian restaurant that she chooses. She's more confident in her own setting, dressed for work, knowing she makes her own way, but she still eyes me with caution. As well she might.

I like spaghetti just fine, so that's what I order in spite of Caroline telling me that in a fancy Italian restaurant like this I should be more adventuresome.

Caroline can't help but know about Wayne's arrest for Dora Lee's murder and the recovery of my Thiebaud. The TV news made a big fuss over both of those things. But they hardly mentioned the theft of the William Kern painting, even though it was the motive for Wayne killing Dora Lee. The Thiebaud was big money. Up beside it, I guess they figured the little Kern landscape was trivial. So, since she's been holed up in Houston, theoretically Caroline shouldn't know a thing about what the Kern was worth.

"You were pretty mysterious on the phone," she says. "Not to mention persistent. I don't mind saying I thought I had put this all behind me."

"I want to discuss the money you'll be getting from your mamma's estate," I say.

"Oh, did Greg decide to sell the farm?"

"No, but he's prepared to buy you out."

"Well, that's good then. Whatever he thinks is fair."

"Don't you wonder how he can afford it?"

She takes a sip of the fine red wine I've ordered. I've become partial to a good glass of red wine. "Why don't you tell me?"

"I think you already know."

She tries to stare me down, but she blinks first. "Things just got out of hand. I didn't think Wayne would go as far as he did."

I look for any sign of distress, but she's dry-eyed and calm. "When did he tell you he'd done it?" I ask.

She takes another sip of wine. It's too good for the likes of her, but it's too late to unorder it. "He came to my place that night. He was a wreck. He hadn't even cleaned the blood off his clothes." She shakes her head, as if talking about a bad child, not a man who killed her mamma.

"I don't understand why he had to kill her. He had the painting. He could have just given her a little bit of money and told her that's all it was worth."

"Oh, believe me, that's exactly what he planned to do. But she found out how much it was really worth."

"From looking it up on the computer?"

"That's right."

I think about the first time I was at Dora Lee's desk and how I didn't bother to open the computer, thinking she probably didn't use it much. If I'd opened it right then, I might have saved myself a fire.

"Who would have suspected that an old country woman like my mother would even have a computer?"

I have to remind myself why Caroline was so bitter toward her mother. It doesn't excuse her part in what was done, but at least it keeps me from telling her what I think of her. "So when your mamma told Wayne she knew what he was up to, he decided to kill her?"

"You make it sound easy, but he told me that he had a hard time deciding what to do. He went out to the farm twice and sat outside trying to work up his courage."

"Courage? That's not a word I'd use to describe a man who stabs a vulnerable old woman in her home."

At least she blushes.

"How did you and Jackson hook up in the first place?" I say.

"I called him about a year ago, after my divorce. I was lonesome one night."

"How'd you know where he was?"

"I called Leslie and he told me."

"So you thought nothing of taking up with a man with a wife and three children."

She shrugs. "He had his choice. I didn't want anything permanent and he knew it."

"At some point he started talking to you about his money worries?"

She nods, sipping the wine, looking at me over the top of the glass. She just can't stop being seductive, even when we're talking about her part in murder and thieving. "He wouldn't shut up about it, worried half to death that Leslie was going to find out he'd lost everything. I remembered that painting. Mother was always going on about it, how it was going to be worth something one day." She shakes her head and her mouth goes all bitter. "I remember once Teague was complaining about the price the cotton crop brought. Mother said, well, if worse comes to worse, we've got that painting. You know what he did?"

I wait. She'll try to win some sympathy by telling me.

"He knocked her down. She had a bowl in her hands, putting our dinner on the table. It broke, and he made her eat it off the floor."

"Don't tell me that." I'm affected, in spite of my revulsion for Caroline.

"You know what still bothers me most about that? Neither Julie nor I made any attempt to help her. We didn't yell at him or beg him, or anything. We just sat there and let it happen. How can one man have managed to get complete control of three women?"

"How old were you?"

"Fourteen? Something like that. Old enough to do *something*."

I don't try to comfort her. My spaghetti comes, but I've lost my appetite.

I thought a lot about what I was going to do with Caroline. If only she had turned in Wayne. Wishful thinking. She may or may not be found guilty of being an accessory to murder and theft. Anyway, I figure no prison is going to keep her locked up the way her upbringing did. I don't like that she'll benefit from the money the painting will bring, but I'm pretty sure there's not enough money in the world to give her a good life. All those things considered, I could have let Caroline's part in the murder slide.

But there's the matter of the little lie she told me to throw me off Wayne's trail. That Wayne had said the painting was sold a long time ago. If she had just let it alone, she might have gotten away with it. I could have argued to myself that she was a victim of Wayne as much as any of us. But that lie told me she knew exactly what Wayne had done.

"What are you going to do with the money from the picture?"

"Quit my job. Maybe go back to California."

She doesn't ask me a thing about her nephew and I don't tell her. I don't feel like tainting his fresh new world with her old, spiteful one.

I've asked Rodell to wait outside the restaurant. He's arranged with the Houston police to take Caroline back to the jail in Bobtail. I'll turn her over to him when we leave. I figure it's best to mend fences with him by giving him this arrest. I just needed to satisfy myself that I was doing the right thing by turning her over. And I'm satisfied.

CHAPTER 29

I'm wishing I could stay away from Houston for a while, but the next week rolls around and it's time to use those baseball tickets I got from Best Land Use Enterprises. The day before the game, Fred Bachman calls to make sure I'm all set up and don't need anything else. He tells me the Four Seasons let him know I had reserved a second room and that his company will be paying for that, too. I tell him it isn't necessary, but he says it's not every day he meets somebody who gives him important information and doesn't want anything in return for it.

Then he tells me their committee met last week and decided to situate the racetrack a few miles further north of Dora Lee's farm, in an area that is flatter and won't need so much excavation. I ask him if it would be appropriate for me to mention this to a few people who might be looking to buy around there. He tells me I can do as I please, that they still have a lot of permits to get before the racetrack happens. "It's all speculation at this point," he says, "so just like any other investment, it involves some risk."

He doesn't mention the Underwoods at all, as if they are erased from his line of sight. Which they might as well be. Rumor has it they've moved on to Dallas and have put their farm up for sale.

I call the real estate outfit in San Antonio that put me onto their trail and have a chat with them about the racetrack in case they might have a need to know. It's fair and square all the way around as far as I'm concerned.

Jenny and I have a fine time in Houston. The Astros win, and the rooms at the Four Seasons are so plush that I feel like I have to tiptoe around in mine. At dinner we work out the details of how Jenny's going to let her horses into the pastureland where I've got the tank, and then we get onto other subjects. We laugh a lot and drink a good bottle of wine and I have a better time than I have in many weeks.

The only awkward time is when we finish our dinner and head for our penthouse floor. Jenny seems a little uneasy on the elevator and I know what it's about. I see her to her door and we stop outside. We both start to say something at the same time. I let her go first.

"This has just been the nicest gift anybody could give me. I just don't want you to think anything more will come of it."

"Jenny, you are a first-rate woman. Getting to know you has been one of those silver linings they talk about in a cloudy situation. But I'm not looking for a girlfriend."

She breaks into a big grin and her cheeks are pink. "If I was out for a man, you'd be right up there at the top."

I give her a kiss on the cheek, not having to bend down far. She's a tall woman. "I'll see you at breakfast."

I don't sleep that well because something has been nagging at the back of my mind, a loose end I haven't wanted to pick up. But the job won't be finished until I do.

A couple of days after the ballgame, when the crew that's going to be putting my house right is set up and ready to begin, I need to get out of there for a few hours. I give Dora Lee's best and oldest friend, Ida Ruth, a call. She tells me she has time to see me this afternoon.

When she opens the door, she says. "I wondered when you would be calling." She leads me inside and sets us up with iced tea and homemade cookies. She goes over and turns off the television before she sits down.

"I'm thinking Dora Lee confided in you," I say, when we are all settled.

"Yes, she did. People don't think an old woman can keep a secret in a small town, but they're wrong." Her eyes glint in defiance, but her voice is tinged with regret.

I am beginning to grasp the truth of that. "I'm trying to make sense out of Dora Lee's story with artist William Kern."

"I guess I can help you with that. Dora Lee once told me if it ever came to it, you're the one person I could talk to. She trusted you, but she couldn't bring herself to tell you what happened."

The story goes back to when Dora Lee's family moved to Austin for a time. Ida Ruth says she doesn't know how they met the artist, William Kern, but he was a frequent visitor in their home. "He was one of those typical starving artists you hear about. Dora Lee's mamma bought the painting from him to tide him over. They didn't have money to speak of, but her mamma was a sweet woman, and she wanted to help him out. If she'd have known what it would lead to, she would have sent him packing."

"So Kern and Dora Lee took up with each other?"

"I don't know that it was like that right away. She was fifteen at the time. All I know is that they did take a shine to each other. After Dora Lee's family moved back here, Dora Lee pined away for him, and he lit out to California for a number of years. So Dora Lee married Teague. I guess you know how that turned out. He was a mean man, no doubt about it."

"That's a fact." I don't know if she is aware of the whole of it, but I'm not about to bring it up.

"Anyway, eventually this Kern fellow came back to Texas. This was in the days when all that 'free love' stuff was going on out in California. When he came back, he brought some of those ideas with him."

I nod, remembering when Jeanne and I went out to San Francisco in the seventies and became aware of social changes we wanted no part of.

The phone rings, but Ida Ruth just looks at it until it stops. "At any rate, Kern came back and got in touch with Dora Lee. She and Teague were married and Caroline was a little girl." She looks at me, as if pleading for me to understand. "It's sometimes hard on a woman living out on a farm, and with somebody like Teague. I expect Dora Lee had kept the idea of this man in the back her mind, him coming to rescue her, some romantic notion. I don't know exactly what happened, whether he called her, or just showed up here. She didn't tell me the details. I didn't really want to hear them. All I know is that Julie was the end result."

I bow my head, thinking that Greg has come by his talent in a way he may never know about. I, for one, will keep it to myself.

Ida Ruth crosses her arms and the scar at the side of her head has reddened. "I don't judge Dora Lee and I hope you don't, either. She was a good friend to me. I try to leave those judgments to the Lord."

Who would have thought this old Baptist woman would take that forgiving attitude? "You were a good friend."

Ida Ruth dabs at her eyes with a tissue. "It was a terrible burden. She couldn't carry it alone. I wisht she hadn't have told me. But I swore I would keep it between her and me, and I did."

"She was awful lucky to have you."

Ida Ruth and I sigh at the same time, and then smile at each other. I wonder in that moment how many secrets lie hidden in our small town that I can't even guess at. We sit for a time, quiet with our own thoughts. Then Ida Ruth's phone rings again and she tells me she's expected down at the church. I can't help thinking what the Reverend Duckworth would make of all this. Maybe I've underestimated him; he might know secrets that he keeps to himself as well.

I get up and put my hat on and tell Ida Ruth I'll see her around. I get in my truck and head back to my place.

The crew that came in to repair the fire damage is well into it now. They say it will take two weeks to finish. I'm planning on having Tom and his family come to see me then. I'll take them to a football game and maybe we'll go eat Mexican food.

I'm looking forward to the time I can start putting my art back into place. There will be new pieces to find a place for. George Manning is sending somebody to bring me that little picture I saw when I was at his gallery. I think Jeanne would have liked it, and she'd like the idea that I'm continuing the interest we pursued together. I'll also be hanging a couple of pictures I bought through George, wanting to help out a certain artist I'm betting will make it big in the future.

ACKNOWLEDGMENTS

The generous support of my fellow writers cannot be exaggerated. Special thanks to my writing buddy Susan Shea, who dispenses encouragement and elegant suggestions. My writing groups critique, praise, and nudge me in the right proportion—thanks to John Gourhan, Martha Jarocki, Ruth Hansell, and Carole Taylor in the Wednesday night mystery writers group; and to my "everything prose" group members—Laird Harrison, Robert Luhn, and Anastasia Hobbett (who is always with us, no matter how far away she is). To the late mystery writer and editor Marilyn Wallace for her unfailing encouragement: you owe me a glass of champagne. And a shout-out to writer Judy Greber for the famous Price Club talk.

Thanks to Sherry Fields, Carol Valk, Mary Ann Boddum, Anne Poirier, and the hiking group—the best cheering squad any writer could have.

Deep appreciation to my agent, Gail Fortune, for believing in me, and to my editor, Dan Mayer, for spinning the brass ring in my direction. This is only the beginning.

A special salute to my grandfather, Sam Gaines, for not going along with the posse. To my dear departed friend Charlie Boldrick, as upright a man as Samuel Craddock, thank you for allowing me to channel your crusty opinions. My love to Geoffrey, a constant source of pride and joy. And abundance of love and appreciation to David, who, along with his many other qualities, indulges my writing habit.

ABOUT THE AUTHOR

TERRY SHAMES grew up in Texas. She has abiding affection for the small town where her grandparents lived, the model for Jarrett Creek. A resident of Berkeley, California, she lives with her husband, two terriers, and an eccentric cat. She is a member of Sisters in Crime and Mystery Writers of America.